Family Promises

Ellie McLellan Genealogy Mystery - Book 3

Beth Farrar

Edited by Ronnie Pelletier

Cover by GetCovers.com

First edition published – 2023

eBook ISBN: 978-1-7386664-6-1

Paperback ISBN: 978-1-7386664-7-8

Hardcover ISBN: 978-1-7386664-8-5

No part of this book was written by AI – just a human's blood, sweat and tears (and some stress!).

Author's Note: Being a Canadian author, please excuse any double "l"s or wayward "u"s in words, eh. Please do not flag them. Much appreciated.

Also By

Ellie McLellan Genealogy Mystery Series

Family Secrets – Book 1

Family Mistakes – Book 2

Contents

To anyone with a dream,
you're never too old to start or complete it.

Never give up!

Chapter One

Notary Bouchard's waiting room was quiet, as quiet as a library, but with comfortable seating and beautiful artwork. Ellie McLellan was there that day for her best friend, Maggie Williams, as Maggie attended the reading of her late grandmother's will. A grandmother she had believed dead for decades. But apparently not.

Ellie had always looked to Maggie for calm and guidance in tough times, but today the roles were reversed. She nudged Maggie's arm. "So, have you decided whether or not to enter the baking contest this year?"

Maggie frowned, as if trying to figure out how the question fit into what was happening at that moment. "The baking contest?"

Ellie squirmed in her seat. She was not a fan of lawyers, no matter how comfortable their chairs were. "Yes, it's about time someone else won."

"No one beats Myrtle Smythe," Maggie said.

"That doesn't mean this can't be your year. But if you don't enter, that blue ribbon will never be pinned up in the Café for all to see."

"There's not much time to come up with something spectacular." Maggie shifted in her seat; the thought having crossed her mind for a fleeting moment before she pushed it away.

Ellie gave Maggie's hand a quick squeeze. "Don't go crazy, just change things up, different flavors or textures. You're fantastic at that."

Before Maggie could respond, the receptionist motioned to them. "Maitre Bouchard will see you now."

"I thought he was a notary," Ellie said a bit too loudly.

The receptionist turned to her and smiled. "Maitre is the French word we use in Quebec for lawyers. Notary or Notaire is a specialized lawyer, and you can address Maitre Bouchard as Notary or Maitre."

"Sounds complicated," Ellie muttered as the receptionist guided them through the open door into an elegant corner office with a breathtaking floor-to-ceiling view of Old Montreal and the sun-dappled St. Lawrence River beyond.

An elderly gentleman stood behind an immaculate desk, a sad smile on his face. "Marguerite, I'm so sorry to meet you like this." His French accent was thick; his English impeccable. He shook hands with them and motioned them toward three chairs in front of his desk.

A knock interrupted the conversation. A man close to their age entered and looked at everyone. "Maitre Bouchard? Je suis ici pour le Will de Octavie Duprat," he said.

"You must be Francois." Notary Bouchard leaned forward to shake the man's hand, and motioned for him to take the empty third seat. "If you don't mind, Francois, Octavie has asked that all meetings be held in English as she wasn't sure Maggie's French was good enough for the legalities. I understand you speak English very well."

Ellie was confused. Who was this Francois, and why was he here? She glanced at Maggie and saw that her friend was just as much in the dark as she was.

Francois sat, his fists jammed in the pockets of his worn-out hoodie, one of his knees jiggling in place. Only then did he look over at the women. They returned his questioning look.

"So." Notary Bouchard leaned forward on his desk. "As you know, Octavie Duprat passed away a few weeks ago. She entrusted me with liquidating her estate and ensuring that all legal aspects of her will were carried out."

"Wait. Who are they?" Francois jerked his chin in their direction.

"I'm sorry, I neglected to introduce you all properly. This is Marguerite, Octavie's granddaughter and..." Notary Bouchard raised an eyebrow at Ellie.

"Ellie McLellan," Ellie replied, looking directly at the unhappy Francois and adding pointedly "best friend and confidant. And you are?"

"I am Octavie's nephew."

"Actually, Francois, you're her great-nephew," Notary Bouchard corrected.

"But she's not allowed here." Francois's eyes snapped from Ellie back to Bouchard. "Is she?"

"Is that a problem?" Notary Bouchard seemed surprised by his comment.

"I asked Ellie to be with me and she's staying," Maggie said, her sole focus on the notary.

"Bon." Notary Bouchard rubbed his hands together and sat back. "We begin." He opened the will and read the contents aloud. From time-to-time he checked with them to make sure they understood everything. When he was finished, he handed Maggie and Francois each a separate document. "This is the inventory of the estate, all noted with valuations. I've followed Octavie's instructions to the letter."

"But," Francois's gaze flew around the office, landing briefly on each of them in turn, refusing to acknowledge the papers in his hand. "Great-Aunt Octavie said she was leaving me...".

"She left you something," Notary Bouchard interrupted. "As you heard when I read the will, you receive thirty thousand dollars and the classic car you have always wanted."

"But she left this..." Francois gestured dismissively towards Maggie, "this...*woman* I've never even *heard of*, everything else! The farm, the bakery, the bank account, the..."

"This woman," Notary Bouchard's voice dropped and became cold, "is Octavie's granddaughter, her blood."

"But I'm blood too!"

"And Octavie left you well provided for." Notary Bouchard held his gaze, daring him to complain further.

Francois grabbed the will and scanned it quickly. "It says '*I leave to my granddaughter, Marguerite*'. Is she even related? Can she prove it? Great-aunt *never* spoke of this person. She could be a... a shyster!"

"Look." Maggie turned to him, her voice calm but her eyes wild with confusion. "I didn't know my grandmother was still alive. This is all news to me—I'm as surprised as you are."

"I doubt it." Francois jumped to his feet and paced the office. "I've helped Great-Aunt for eight years, doing anything she asked, helping her with whatever she needed. She was very demanding, but she told me I'd—"

Notary Bouchard held up his hand. "Francois, Octavie was very clear about how she wanted her estate divided."

"She must have been too ill to know what she was doing." Francois resumed his seat and leaned forward, pleading his case. "Maybe she had dementia and forgot what she—"

Again, the notary interrupted. "Octavie made her will two years ago. When she died, she was of sound mind and body, just as she was when she made the will. Octavie was fully aware of what she owned and who she wanted to leave it to. She did not share with me *why* she made those decisions, but I *will* see that they are carried out."

Francois glared at Maggie and snapped, "You didn't even come to her funeral!"

"I didn't even know she was alive, let alone dead!" Maggie blurted out, her composure evaporating. Ellie gave Maggie's hand a quick squeeze, hoping to keep her in the present. She was relieved to see Maggie relax in her chair, take a deep breath, and deliberately turn away from Francois. She focused her attention back to Notary Bouchard.

Ellie glanced furtively at Francois. What did this make him? She pictured a general family tree in her mind. He would be Maggie's second cousin.

Maggie whispered, "Did she know she was going to die?"

"She did," Notary Bouchard sighed, his gaze softening on Maggie. "But she thought she had a little more time. Octavie and I had been close friends since childhood, and we trusted each other in everything. She was a perfectionist about her security, her money, her wellbeing. Octavie was careful not to burden those she left behind with details and legal issues. I wish all my clients were like that!"

He reached into a drawer and pulled out a key ring with at least ten keys dangling from it. The keys jingled as he handed them to Maggie. "These fit everything that belonged to Octavie. Her house, her barn, any other building she owned, or anything that needed to be kept safe. The address of her property is on the document I gave you. You are free to go there at any time."

Francois's loud gasp filled the room. Ellie stiffened, steeling herself against another outburst.

Notary Bouchard turned to him. "And I will ask you to return any keys Octavie gave you, as you no longer have free access to the property."

Francois jumped to his feet, crushing the inventory document in his fist, and headed for the door. He spat, "She never gave me any keys."

"Wait," Notary Bouchard called after him.

Francois spun around, his eyes black holes of anger.

"It will take time for all the legalities to be processed. As soon as they are completed, I will notify you of the transfer of your share of the estate."

Francois's dark gaze swept over Maggie, his eyes narrowed to daggers. Wordlessly he shook his head and stalked out of the room, slamming the door behind him.

"Well," Ellie said, releasing the deep breath she'd been holding in. "That went well."

***

Half an hour later, Maggie and Ellie were sitting on a bench by the river, ham and cheese sandwiches between them, watching the boats drift by. Seagulls swooped around, waiting for pieces of bread Maggie tossed their way. Their cries were high and shrill, as if calling to each other that there was food here.

Maggie pushed back a wind-blown strand of hair. "So, how am I related to Francois?"

Ellie could see that Maggie was still processing everything she'd learned. As a genealogist by trade, Ellie's skills would come in handy today, and especially in this case, as family relations were her passion. She brushed crumbs from her lap as she explained the family connection. "Francois called her great-aunt, so that would make him your second cousin, which means one of his grandparents is a sibling of your grandmother's."

"Ellie." Maggie held her sandwich with disinterest. "I don't need this in my life right now. It's so..."

"Exciting!" Ellie leaned in and gave her a sideways nudge. "Imagine, you found a grandmother, you inherited—well, we're not sure exactly what you inherited—but it sounds amazing."

Maggie countered, "And I have a relative who hates me!"

"Yeah, we'll have to..." Ellie stuttered to a halt, shocked to see the subject of their conversation stalking down the tree-lined path toward them.

Without preamble, Francois planted himself in front of them and said, "We need to talk about this." He stood over Maggie, aggressively invading her space.

Ellie jumped to her feet, stepping between him and Maggie, forcing him to step back.

Maggie dropped her sandwich on the bench and stood beside her friend. "There's nothing to talk about."

"Obviously there is because Great-Aunt promised to leave everything to me."

"But she didn't," Ellie said.

"This has nothing to do with you," he snapped, dismissing her with a sidestep, his eyes glued to Maggie's pale face. He clenched his fists, and puffed out his chest. "How can you accept this inheritance when you had nothing to do with her life? You did *nothing* for her. *I* looked after her and the farm. You don't belong to this family."

Ellie pushed her five-foot-two body in front of him once again, hands on her hips, forcing him to deal with her. "Maggie is her grandmother's blood. She belongs. Her grandmother *made* her belong. And for whatever reason she wrote her will the way she did, you have to accept it. I think I understand her reasons now."

As he reached to push her aside, Maggie surprised him—and Ellie—by grabbing his hand and twisting his thumb until a spear of pain shot across his face. "Don't touch her," she growled before letting him go. They all backed away from each other.

"Hey, I'm sorry." His voice did not match his words, his anger plain to see. "This is a shock to me."

"To all of us," Maggie said. She rubbed at the sudden goosebumps on her arms, perhaps frightened by her instinctive reaction to Francois's aggression.

Maggie was a gentle woman and lived a gentle life. Seeing her like this made Ellie furious.

"We're done here." Ellie picked up their half-eaten sandwiches and threw them in the trash. "When you threaten people, there are consequences!"

"This is not over," Francois called after them as they walked away. "Not by a long shot. I'll get what I deserve."

Chapter Two

"What could he do?" Maggie asked from the passenger seat on the hour-long drive home.

Ellie glanced at her and saw that she was clenching her jaw, still shaken by the physical aspect of her encounter with her cousin. Ellie reached out and grabbed one of Maggie's flailing hands, and gave it a quick squeeze, before resuming her two-fisted death grip on the steering wheel. "Mags, this is quite a mystery, but we'll figure it out."

Maggie slumped in her seat. "I can hardly believe it—I own a farm and a bakery somewhere." She peered into the document envelope for the hundredth time, this time pulling out the sheet of paper with the address. "Where is St. Anne de Lafont? I've never heard of that place. No, wait! I have. It's where the Tavie Bakery is located. Or as it's called in French, Boulangerie Tavie. We learned about it in school." She stared at the paper in her hands and whispered, "No. It can't be."

Ellie glanced briefly from the road to the paper. A shaky hand had written the note, and it seemed logical that Notary Bouchard had written it. Not what she'd expected from the notary, but at the bottom she caught a glimpse of an unexpected little heart with a smiley face in the middle.

Maggie asked, "Can you imagine Notary Bouchard drawing hearts and smiley faces on things for clients?"

Ellie laughed, checked her mirrors again, and left the highway for a longer route through the back roads. She hated the daredevils on the highway, and they weren't in a hurry. "No, he doesn't strike me as the emoji type at all."

"Then my grandmother wrote this," Maggie scanned the papers in her hands, "and she was Tavie!"

"You mean the famous Boulangerie Tavie?" Ellie used the French pronunciation with a roll of her tongue.

Maggie nodded. "It's in St. Anne de Lafont, and when Notary Bouchard told us she owned a bakery, I mean, how many bakeries does a small town have? And Tavie could be short for Octavie."

"So, you're going to be Tavie Bakery?"

"Heavens no!" Maggie recoiled at the thought. "I don't need that kind of stress. It's a substantial business, but ... no." She checked the note again, overwhelmed by the thought of what she had inherited. "No, I love my Cozy Corner Café and that's all I need, or want."

They drove in silence for a while, each thinking about the revelations that lay ahead. Ellie broke the silence. "So, what about Francois?"

Maggie dragged her glance back from the fields beyond the window and made a face at Ellie. "Nothing. I'll wait for Notary Bouchard to finish his job, and that's it."

"And how's it going with Pete?"

"Nice change of subject. It's good, thanks." Maggie took a deep breath. "His parents are just as wonderful as you said, though Pete is moving faster than your Scottish giant."

"It's mutually beneficial, for now."

"You're not getting any younger."

"Says the woman who's older than me."

"Which is why I'm enjoying all that life has to offer," Maggie said. "And at our age, one year older is nothing."

"Can you stop at my place for a few minutes and talk to Quinn about this?" Ellie urged as they neared home. "Francois gave me the creeps, and I want to find out what Quinn thinks about it. Remember, he *was* a police officer."

"In Scotland," Maggie said. "But sure. And you never answered my question. How is Prince Charming?"

"He *is* rather a Prince Charming, isn't he?" Ellie was in the early stages of a full-blown romance with Quinn, and she knew that Maggie took great pleasure in seeing her happy after Ellie lost her husband and daughter in a car accident a few years earlier. Ellie and Quinn's meeting was the stuff of romance novels, and over the course of a few short months, they had become inseparable.

"So, why *are* you and Quinn still taking it slow?" Maggie asked as they drove up Ellie's driveway and passed the barn that Quinn had rented from Ellie for his furniture business.

Quinn stepped out at the sound of the car, and waved; Cali, Ellie's golden-brown retriever, at his side. Ellie parked and whispered to Maggie. "Right now, slow as molasses is the way to go, but I'm not sure how long that's going to last." She hesitated before opening the door. "He's such a good kisser!"

***

Ellie and Quinn sat on the swing on the porch while Maggie took one of the steps below. Excited at Ellie's return, Cali moved back and forth between Ellie and Quinn, delivering wet licks before Ellie motioned for her to lie down. "So, we're hoping you have some advice," Ellie said after filling Quinn in on the visit to the notary and their encounter with Francois.

Quinn stretched his long legs out in front of him. "About the legal stuff, or about cousin Francois?"

Maggie tossed Cali's fetch toy, then watched the dog leap from the porch after it. "I like Notary Bouchard, and I trust him to do what needs to be done. But Francois, I have a bad feeling about him."

"You can't do anything about him unless he threatens you or commits a crime," Quinn said.

Ellie left Quinn's side to sit down next to her friend. She slid her arm through Maggie's, hoping some of her calm would trickle down to her. "Look at it this way, he must live up north, near your grandmother. And I can't see him driving all that way and back each day if he lived around here."

"True," Maggie leaned into Ellie. "He seemed as surprised as I was at the turn of events."

"Turn of events?" Ellie laughed. "Have you been reading old detective stories?"

"Someone left an Agatha Christie in the Café's bathroom, of all places." Maggie grinned. "And it wasn't one from the Café's book collection." Maggie hesitated, then said. "Ellie, should I get my papers together to prove who I am? Just in case?"

"I don't think you'll need to, but if it makes you feel better, sure." Ellie watched the emotions cross Maggie's face and the worry reach her eyes. "Get your birth certificate, your parents' marriage certificate, and your mother's birth certificate. That should do it, *if* you need it at all."

Quinn stood and stretched. "Ladies, I'd love to stay and jabber, but I have to get back to work."

They faced him; eyes wide with surprise. "Jabber?" Ellie sputtered. "Is that your new word of the day?"

He reached for her and dropped a kiss on the top of her head. "Just trying to get a rise out of you." She punched him in the arm, which he grabbed and moaned in feigned pain.

He disappeared into the barn, and Cali returned to her spot at their feet, dropping her toy in front of them. Maggie picked it up but didn't throw it, obviously distracted. "Ellie, do you have a few minutes to do a quick search on my grandmother? See if we can find anything?" She checked her watch. "I've got about half an hour."

Ellie jumped up and pulled Maggie to her feet. "Let's go. Time's a wasting!"

Once seated at the kitchen table, Ellie opened her computer and frowned. "So, I think the best thing to do is just Google Boulangerie Tavie. See what pops up." Her fingers flew over the keyboard.

Maggie pulled her chair closer and squinted at the screen. "Oh, look! There's a Wikipedia page!"

Ellie opened the page and they were disappointed to see how little information was displayed. "Well, it's located in St. Anne de Lafont."

"Which we knew."

"Opened after the war by Octavie Duprat."

"But it doesn't say anything else about *her*," Maggie said.

"She must have been a private person."

Maggie slumped back in her seat. "Even *I* didn't know who she was!"

Ellie flipped back to the main search page and scrolled through the entries. "Here's the company website." The page opened to reveal a minimalist site.

Maggie reached out and touched the link to the About page. "This is rather low-key. Her brand is huge in Quebec, but her production is not."

"She has a walk-in bakery," Ellie read further, "and she sells to a few specialty shops. Most of this looks like online orders though."

"That can't be," Maggie said. "I bought a box of her chocolate chip cookies at IGA the other day."

"You bought someone else's cookies?" Ellie looked shocked.

Maggie shrugged her shoulders. "So, sue me. They're delicious. But now that I think about it, that's the only item of hers in the store. No, there were macaroons too."

"Maybe they are easy to make in larger quantities. She must have had a reason for keeping her business small."

"Okay," Maggie sat forward again. "What else can we find?"

"Wait a second. I want to take a screenshot," Ellie said. "If you have a record of it that way, you can go back later and take your time reading it without having to search for it again. I'll do that with everything we find. That way we won't go back to something we've already seen. And yes, you can just Google everything later, but I like records."

"What about census returns?" Maggie asked.

"Well, her business wouldn't be listed on any available census return, but she might be listed with her family. Let's check the 1921 census and see what we can find."

"What are we looking at?" Maggie's eyes were all over the site and what it offered.

"Library and Archives Canada. There are other sites where you can search for census records, but this is free and fast for Canada. England and the US have amazing returns, by the way, and I use Ancestry and Family Search, among others." Ellie murmured the last comment in delight as she typed in the search information and waited for the results.

"Wow," Maggie said quietly. "That's a lot of Duprats in St. Anne de Lafont. How will we know which one is ours?

"There are no specific Octavies noted, so maybe she wasn't born yet," Ellie said. "And since we don't know what her parents' names were, we need to talk to Notary Bouchard again. I'm sure he'll know."

Maggie looked at the clock and started to fidget. "Can we check a few more things?"

"At this point, I'd look at the Drouin collection, as they have a huge deposit of records for births, marriages, and deaths. But since we don't know when your grandmother was born, or who her parents were, I don't think you have the time right now to search without more information."

"And just because her bakery is in St. Anne de Lafont, that doesn't mean she was born there, right?" Maggie asked.

"Very good point."

"So, we'll come back to that. What about city directories?" Maggie asked. "We know for a fact that the bakery was in St. Anne de Lafont."

Ellie returned to typing. "The town is rather small, so I'll have to go into Family Search or the National Library of Canada to dig deeper to find the area where records would be."

"I don't have time for that right now."

"Okay," Ellie said as she returned to the computer. "How about ..." After a few keystrokes, she sat back so Maggie could see the screen.

"What's this?" Maggie looked at the picture of her grandmother attached to a death announcement.

"I did a quick Google search for her obituary, typed in her name, the words obituary and Quebec, and this is what came up."

"I wonder why she's listed in the Montreal Gazette. That's a bit far from St. Anne de Lafont."

"Perhaps she left instructions to do so, maybe so you could find it," Ellie said, loving the possibility.

"She looks just like the picture on her baked goods. The obituary names the town, but not where she was born, or how old she was when she died."

"I have a feeling Notary Bouchard dealt with this. Wait, let me take a screenshot of it."

"I still have ten minutes," Maggie said, checking her watch once again. "I know this can take some time, all this searching and stuff, but..."

Ellie shook her head in pretend disgust. "All this searching and stuff? Jeesh, Maggie, that's ..."

"I know, I know!" Maggie held up her hands to ward off Ellie's words. "It's like being a detective, which can take a bit of time. And you know I'm not patient, but I'm working on that character flaw."

"That I'd like to see," Ellie said, turning back to the computer. "Okay. One more quick thing. I'm going to check out the BGSU University Libraries website. Here we go, Historical Canadian Newspapers online, and I'm going to ask specifically for Quebec. I love searching this site, and it's free. There are other sites that offer newspaper searching, but let's just do a quick search for now. This one, Le Progres du Richelieu, January 31, 1952, would have been a newspaper in the St. Anne de Lafont area. And it only cost five cents at the time!" She enlarged the pages and flipped through them. "Here, look at the last page at the bottom. There's a small advertisement for Boulangerie Tavie. It's in French, so let me translate it. It says "*Fresh baked goods daily at reasonable prices. Visit our little town and enjoy the scenery and a pastry.*".

"I wonder how much that cost!" Maggie said. "So, we know she was in business in 1952, and that's seven years after the war ended. I guess she must have been doing well to be able to afford an advertisement."

"Let me take a screenshot of that too. There's probably more but..."

Quinn walked in as they finished. They stood up from the table and Ellie closed her computer. "Are you two hens still chatting?"

The women gave him a look that made him step back and laugh.

"We found a lot of information," Ellie informed him.

"Good enough for a start," Maggie said, gathering her things. "We'll see how it goes. But for now, I have to run," Maggie grabbed Ellie for a quick hug of thanks. She tossed them a wave as she headed for the path that led through the woods, across the highway, and to her Cozy Corner Café.

"Maggie," Quinn called after her.

She stopped and looked back.

"I wouldn't worry. Your notary has everything under control, and once the shock wears off, your cousin will come to his senses."

Maggie weighed Quinn's words and nodded.

"And I'll come by the Café more often if you want," Ellie said. "Make sure you're okay. And maybe have a cookie."

"Bye guys, pastries await." She turned and disappeared into the forest, whistling "I'm Dreaming of a White Christmas".

"She knows it's the middle of summer, right?" Quinn asked Ellie as the tune faded.

"It's her coping mechanism." Ellie wrapped her arm around his waist and looked up at him. "We all have them, and hers is pretty entertaining."

Quinn bent, kissed her quick, hugged her tight, then deliberately set her away from him. "I really need to get to work, and you're such a distraction." He swooped in for another kiss and she wrapped her arms around his neck. "Distraction, distraction, distraction," he whispered against her lips.

But it was Ellie who pulled away first. "Come on Cali, time to blow off some steam!" She grabbed Cali's toy from the ground and dashed off into the woods. She turned to see Cali and Quinn looking at each other, as if wondering what was wrong with her.

Chapter Three

Maggie had left the Cozy Corner Café that morning in the capable hands of her second-in-command, Daphne, and returned around two o'clock to the quiet afternoon lull.

"Hey," Daphne said as she came out of the kitchen, retying her long blond hair into a manageable ponytail. "How did it go?"

Inside her head, Maggie toyed with a response, hardly believing the words she was about to say. "My grandmother didn't die years ago, and she was the Tavie Bakery." She took her apron from a hook by the door and tied it on.

"Yeah, right," Daphne laughed at her, then stopped short when she saw Maggie's face. "You mean Tavie Bakery, as in Boulangerie Tavie, the best pastries this side of the Atlantic Ocean?"

"That's right," Maggie said. "And those two facts surprise the heck out of me, that no one told me my grandmother was still alive, and she was Tavie Bakery."

"How did you not know she was alive? Didn't your parents ever..."

"My mother told me she died years ago." Maggie washed her hands, then hesitated, water still running over her motionless fingers, then turned to Daphne with a puzzled expression. "Why in the world would she tell me her own mother had died?"

Daphne shrugged.

Maggie turned off the water and shook her head. "I've got things to do right now. I'll think about it more tomorrow."

"Do what you do, Scarlett," Daphne said as she emptied the dishwasher.

"La De Da," Maggie replied, acknowledging the younger woman's reference to Gone with the Wind. "How was the morning?"

For the next few minutes, the two women discussed business, then parted to do their own chores for the afternoon. Maggie made an assortment of sandwiches to go along with the pastries for the supper crowd of tourists and locals, and Daphne cleaned the dining area and back room. Maggie believed that a spotless cafe gave her customers confidence in her food, so she never skimped on the cleaning.

When the front door swung open an hour later, Maggie was taking a break at a table, a cup of coffee and a pastry in front of her. Shirley Cooper, a 93-year-old senior from Ellie's genealogy group, shuffled over and put a file on the table before sitting down across from her.

"Phew," she let out a breath. "I should have driven over. But Ruth's right, it's great exercise to walk!"

Daphne appeared at her side with an iced tea and a couple of macaroons, Shirley's favorite dessert.

"Oh, you are such a sweetheart," Shirley said to Daphne. She took a grateful sip of the tea and a quick bite of her pastry before opening her folder with a flourish and smiling at Maggie.

"You look like the cat that caught the mouse," Maggie said, popping a piece of her croissant into her mouth.

Shirley turned the file around for Maggie to see. "I have a plan. We can do something special for the front of the Café, not expensive, but colorful and inviting."

Shirley had found a hobby ten years ago that she had recently turned into a lucrative business. She was a mini landscaper. That is, she would do small jobs for people, whether it was tidying up a flower bed, adding accents to the front of a house, or just consulting, her services had become quite in demand. She had a real flair and eye for color, function, and proportion, and she had become well-known and sought after. Whenever the work was too strenuous, she hired someone to help her part-time. It worked well for her.

Maggie pulled the file closer and turned the pages, revealing wooden benches, bird baths, and window boxes. "Shirley," she said, "it just so happens that I've just received an inheritance from my grandmother. Totally unexpected."

If Shirley was surprised by the change of subject, she didn't show it. Instead, she perked up and leaned forward with bright eyes. "I thought your grandmother died a long time ago?"

"So did I." Maggie tapped her fingers over the glossy pictures in the file and shrugged. "Seems I was wrong. I'm not telling everyone this, but my grandmother was Tavie Bakery."

"What?" Shirley jerked back in surprise. "But Tavie Bakery is a Quebec legend. She built her bakery from nothing to..." She hesitated. "You mean your *grandmother* was Tavie?"

"That's what I said."

"And you didn't know?" Shirley seemed confused.

"No," Maggie said quietly, realizing how this must sound. "My mother told me she died a long time ago. I don't know why she told me that, but now I have to deal with my grandmother's estate for the next few months."

Shirley blinked at her and considered her words. "Then I'm sure you don't want to start all this, dear." Shirley gathered up the pages and put them back in her folder. "You'll have enough—"

"On the contrary." Maggie reached out and stopped her. "I love my café as much as my grandmother loved her business. I'm going to invest a little more in this place than I had originally planned. Let's see what you have in mind.

***

The women's heads were bent together over the folder when Shirley's sister, Ruth, entered the Café a short time later. They saw her and waved, but continued their discussion while Ruth ordered pastries to go from Daphne.

With her bag in hand, Ruth approached them and leaned against the back of a chair. "And what are you two plotting?" Her smile softened the question.

"I'm sprucing up the Café," Maggie said. "And Shirley is designing it for me."

"I'm glad you finally agreed to it," Shirley said.

"You wore me out."

"You couldn't be in better hands," Ruth smiled at her sister. "I'm going to visit Ellie for a bit." She held the bag out for them to see, as if that explained everything.

"Getting her sugar fix, is she?" Maggie laughed, since most people knew about Ellie's sweet tooth.

"And I'm getting my daily meander," Ruth said.

"Should I pick you up later?" Shirley asked.

Ruth hesitated, still unsure of the new relationship they had formed over the last month. Shirley no longer hovered over her every second, the beginning of forgiveness on both sides for past indiscretions still on shaky ground. It felt good not to have to sneak over to visit Ellie, but it would take some getting used to. "Sure," she agreed.

"Perfect," Shirley said. "I'll run into town to pick up my flower order and swing by for you on the way back."

***

Ruth left them chatting about the best shades of flowers for the window boxes, and walked across the street and into the woods. Ellie kept the path hidden, but accessible for Ruth to walk through whenever she wanted to stop by.

Once upon a time, Ruth and Shirley had owned Ellie's house. They had grown up there, but had sold it to Ellie and her husband several years earlier when the sisters realized that the farmhouse had become too much for them. It had been heartbreaking for Ruth because she felt she had left her heart in that house. But the sisters had moved across the highway to the Tiny House Haven community, behind the Cozy Corner Café, and were now living in a smaller, more manageable home.

She passed the treehouse and stopped to run her fingers across the carved initials her one and only love, Jeremy, had carved before he left for the war in early 1945. Clutching her bag tighter, she made her way through the woods to the farmhouse.

The sound of hammering from the barn alerted her that Quinn was working on another project for his handcrafted furniture business. A smile played across Ruth's lips; pleased that Ellie had finally let someone into her life.

"Ruth!" Ellie flung open the front screen door and bounded down the stairs to meet her. She pulled the tiny woman into a gentle hug, then turned her nose to the bag in the woman's hand. "What is that I smell?"

"Treats for the both of us, and something for Quinn." Ruth accepted Ellie's assistance up the stairs and into the house.

"Is the walk getting too hard in this heat?" Ellie asked as she gathered some plates for the pastries and sat down at the kitchen table.

"A little," Ruth admitted. "But I'm not sleeping as well as I should these days." She opened the bag and put all the pastries on the plate.

"Spending too much time with Jeremy?" Ellie reached for an éclair and took a small bite, stifling the groan of pleasure Maggie's baking always brought.

"I can never spend too much time with him," Ruth said. "He's going in for his surgery tomorrow, and I plan to visit him every day to help with his recovery."

"He's lucky to have you," Ellie said between bites. She looked down at her plate in mock surprise that the whole éclair was gone, which made Ruth laugh.

"I think we're both lucky," Ruth said.

"And how is Shirley handling you spending so much time away from her?"

Ruth finished her croissant and wiped her mouth. "She's been super busy ever since she took that contract from Sara for the Tiny House Haven's landscaping. It's the biggest job she's ever had. She's also working at Maggie's, and Phil has something he wants done at his place as well. She doesn't miss me."

"And how do you feel about that?"

Ruth knew that Ellie was watching her closely. Ruth and her sister were both feeling their way forward, and learning that being in their nineties was not the end of the world after all. "Wonderful," she said.

Cali sat next to Ruth, accepting the tiny pieces of pastry that Ruth secretly passed to her. The dog's head whipped around when she heard heavy boots on the porch. She ran to greet Quinn, her tail wagging vigorously as he strolled in.

He eyed the plate and the lone doughnut it held, raising an eyebrow. "I sure hope that one's mine." He planted a quick kiss on the top of Ellie's head.

Ruth beamed. Here were two of her favorite people, and they had their whole lives ahead of them. "Indeed it is." Ruth slid the donut toward him and shook her head in amazement as he devoured it in three bites. "Don't forget to breathe once in a while!"

"Sorry, Ruth," he said. "That was rude, but I was getting hangry. That hit the spot."

A car pulled up in the driveway. "That will be my ride," Ruth stood up awkwardly. It had been a long hot day, and tomorrow promised to be even more exhausting as she waited for Jeremy's knee surgery to be completed. Quinn offered her his hand, which she gratefully accepted, and rested on his arm as they walked through the house and out to the car.

"Give Jeremy my best for tomorrow," Ellie called after her.

Ruth gave a slight nod of acknowledgement and let Quinn help her into the passenger seat. The sisters both waved and drove down the road with Cali running a short distance to see them off.

Chapter Four

When she closed the Café at seven that night, Maggie's entire body ached with fatigue and lingering stress. The emotions she'd experienced between the meeting with the notary and her newfound cousin's attitude, including an influx of tourists who cleaned out her pastries, had left her exhausted.

With the doors locked and the lights off on the ground floor, she walked up the narrow stairs to her living quarters above. Maggie's home was her sanctuary, her refuge, and a destination for comfort after a hard day's work.

The Cozy Corner Café had originally been a farmhouse, built over a hundred and fifty years ago. When Maggie bought it, the building needed renovations to bring it up to code so she could run her business on the main floor. But upstairs, where the five bedrooms and a bathroom were, she had taken her time renovating to her taste. And her taste had been to keep things as original as possible.

She took down a few walls to make her bedroom and living room larger. And she updated the bathroom, including the fixtures, though the claw-foot tub remained after receiving a fresh coat of red paint. Since she used the Café's kitchen on the main floor whenever the mood struck, her private kitchen was minimalist for her personal needs. She loved to make small batches of treats for herself and friends in her home kitchen. She never tired of baking, and after today's revelation, she now understood why; it was in her blood.

The day Maggie signed the deed to the Cozy Corner Café was the moment her dream of owning her own bakery came true. She'd searched far and wide for the perfect location, but it was Ellie who found the building for sale, across the highway from her own home. She immediately called Maggie while standing in front of the realtor's sign. Within days, the deal was done, and they were in the building's bare main room, squealing with excitement, not only because Maggie was going to open her Cafe, but the distance between the best friends was now just a literal walk through Ellie's woods.

The year after the purchase passed quickly. Maggie's reputation for French pastries had her delights selling out by the end of each day, and her side-business of catering for parties was growing by word of mouth. She felt more at home in the town of Percyville, with a small group of friends, than ever before in her life.

The sun streamed through the trees as she looked out the back at the Tiny House Haven homes in the distance. The lake, surrounded by these pretty little homes, glistened in the fading light and sparkled as if magical fairies were gliding across its surface.

Maggie changed out of her work clothes and slipped into a bright knee length caftan. The heat of the day had subsided, her windows were open wide, and a breeze caught her dress as she gathered her personal papers from a tall cabinet in the living room.

She placed them on the kitchen table and sat down to begin her search. What had Ellie said she needed? Her birth certificate, her parents' marriage license, and her mother's birth certificate.

She found her own birth certificate in her "special things" envelope, and spread it out, reading each notation. Marguerite Catherine Williams, born September 9, 1989 at three-thirteen a.m. Florence Duprat, mother, and Luke Williams, father. She winced as she imagined her poor mother laboring through the night. She sat back with the paper in her hand, lost in thought and missing her mother. The last five years without her had been hard on her and her father.

What would her mother think of her inheritance? And how would she explain keeping Maggie away from her grandmother?

She set the birth certificate aside, tipped the envelope over and emptied the rest of the contents onto the table. She shifted through the report cards, concert tickets, theatre bills, and other miscellaneous memories of her life, but found nothing more of importance.

Something had been nagging at her in the back of her mind. She grabbed her grandmother's will and opened it to the first page. Studying her birth certificate again, she noticed that her mother's maiden name was also Duprat.

She grabbed her phone and speed dialed Ellie, and before her friend could even say hello, Maggie blurted out, "Don't women in Quebec use their maiden names on all legal documents?"

"Hello to you too," Ellie said. "Can you give me some details here?"

"Sorry." Maggie took a deep breath and collected herself. "Well, my birth certificate says my parents are Florence Duprat and Luke Williams. Those are facts."

"Correct."

"But," Maggie continued, "my grandmother's will says her name is Octavie Duprat. There is no indication anywhere that Octavie was married and the Duprat name is her husband's name. So, the Duprat last name is the same as my mom, which can't be, because mom would have her father's name. Right?"

"Usually."

"What do you mean, usually? Have you ever come across a case where a child had their mother's name?" Ellie didn't answer. "There's no father, right?"

"Well," Ellie said, "do you have your parents' marriage license? It could have both of their parents' names on it, but your mother's birth certificate would be even better."

"I don't have them, but I'll ask Dad if he does."

"Sounds like this is turning into a bit of a mystery," Ellie joked.

"True, but what if this mystery turns out to be something that prevents me from inheriting?" Maggie's voice rose an octave, as she realized she quite liked the idea of being her grandmother's heir.

"First things first," Ellie said. "See what your dad has, and then we'll go from there."

"Right. Sorry to bother you, El. I know you're busy with your genealogy book."

"I'm almost done." Ellie let out a sigh, and Maggie imagined her stretching her arms out and then curling up back over her computer to finish the task. "There are so many elements regarding interviewing relatives, and I don't want to miss anything. But anyway, keep me posted on what you find out, okay?"

"Done," Maggie said. "Thanks."

"Anytime."

Without skipping a beat, Maggie hung up and dialed another number. "Dad?" she said. "How are you?" They spent the next few minutes in small talk, catching up on the days since they had last spoken, until she finally got to the reason for her call. "Can I come and see you tomorrow? I went to the notary today and I have a lot of questions. I'll explain everything when I get there."

Luke was a man of few words when a mystery presented itself, preferring to have facts in front of him. But he told her to drop by and he'd have a cup of tea waiting. Ringing off, Maggie sat with the phone cradled in her hands.

Her father had been stunned when she had first told him about the impending visit to the notary regarding her grandmother's will. He, too, believed that Octavie had died years ago, and his silence on the phone was perhaps an indication that he realized his wife had lied to him. This upset Maggie. The last person who deserved more pain was her father.

Maybe the two of them could put the pieces of this puzzle together and solve this mystery.

Chapter Five

Maggie finished the baking for the day, stocked the display cases with pastries, and posted the sandwich menu on the board at the counter, all before Daphne strolled through the door at 6:45.

"Jeesh Louise," the young woman mumbled as she reached for her personal mug and filled it to the brim with dark, delicious wake-up coffee. "Did you sleep at all?"

"I did." Maggie removed her apron and washed her hands before turning to her second-in-command. "I have to go out for an hour or so, but everything's ready for the morning rush."

"You're lucky it's the slowest time of the week." Daphne joked as she took another sip from her mug, then tied on her apron before inspecting the contents of the pastry cases and the day's menu. "Looks good." With concern on her face, she reached out to stop Maggie before she headed out the door. "But what's going on? Are you sure you're okay?"

Maggie smiled, the first smile she'd shown since returning from the notary's office, and nodded. "I think I am. I'm going to see my dad. Hopefully he can fill in some blanks for me. But I won't be long." She hurried out, the bell tinkling as the door closed behind her.

***

Luke Williams lived on the outskirts of Percyville, at the opposite end from Ellie's farm and the Cozy Corner Café. It took Maggie only ten minutes to drive the winding roads to the house where her parents had retired.

Fifty years ago, the original owners had built it in a century-old style. Illness forced them to sell quickly, and Luke and Florence had snapped it up when Maggie left for university and their Montreal home became too big. It was similar to Ellie's farmhouse, but on a smaller scale, and there was a room waiting for Maggie whenever she wanted to come visit while she was at school.

She and Ellie met at university, and Maggie was surprised to learn that Ellie had grown up in the town where her parents had settled. The two women became inseparable from their very first meeting. Their friends referred to them as Mutt and Jeff, Maggie being tall and red-haired, while Ellie was tiny and dark-haired.

Her dad waited at the door, his arms open wide for the deep hug they always shared. "It's good to see you," he said, reluctantly releasing her and motioning her into the house.

Maggie stopped short at the entrance to the living room, taking in the new leather recliner in the corner facing the television. "You've upgraded."

Luke eased past her to stand beside his new pride and joy. "My back told me to get something firmer."

"I'm sure your back gave you good advice." She smiled at him. Neither made a move to sit, so Maggie dove in. "Dad, did you know Mom's mother was still alive?"

He hesitated a fraction, as if unsure of his memory. "Florence told me she had no siblings, and her mother died when Florence moved to Montreal. Other than that, I don't remember her ever talking about her family."

"Didn't that seem odd?"

"Not really. I was in the same boat, an only child, no relatives to speak of. I guess that's part of what drew us together at university." He stared off, deep in thought. "We were looking forward, not back."

"I have to admit I'm angry about this," Maggie said, embarrassed by her feelings. "I would have loved to have had a grandmother, or some other family! Well, there might be more out there, or at least this second cousin, Francois character—he was at the reading of the will yesterday—not someone you'd want to meet, believe me. But—there *could* be more out there."

"Maybe Ellie could look for them?" Luke smiled at her. He knew how proud she was of her friend's ability to help others.

"Perhaps." Maggie nodded. "But for now, I'm going to take this one step at a time."

"To be honest, I feel betrayed that your mother lied to me," he admitted.

"She must have had a reason, Dad." Maggie put her arm around his shoulders. He seemed older; frail. When had that happened? "Mom loved you more than anything, including me."

"Oh, I don't know about that." He turned and linked his arm with hers. They stood together in their favorite spot, looking out the large picture window at the woods beyond the property. During her visits, they spent many nights either curled up on the couch looking out in winter, or sprawled out on the balcony in the summer. Even though Maggie was a grown woman when they bought this house, Luke had continued to spin fairy tales similar to those he had when Maggie was a child. She treasured them all.

When Maggie had been younger, Florence had scolded him for some of the scarier tales—but those were the ones Maggie loved the most.

Maggie stepped back, hauled her backpack from the floor, and pulled out her birth certificate. "Well, this is all I have. I've got mine, but did mom keep hers here, and do you have your marriage certificate around, by any chance?"

Luke frowned at her. "I would have to go through the box of papers your mother kept. Do you need them right now?"

Maggie noticed the concern on his face, and the last thing she wanted to do was worry her father. She should have mentioned exactly what she was looking for the night before. "No, no, the next few days would be great. And if you can't find them, I'll check with Ellie and see what else we can do. She doesn't think I need them, but I want a copy for myself, anyway."

Luke nodded and made his way to the couch, sitting down and patting the seat next to him. "Come. Tell me all about this inheritance and what you're going to do with it. Sounds like it's going to be quite an adventure."

They spent the next hour discussing the will, the discovery of who Tavie Bakery was, and what Maggie might do in the future. She left out the part about Francois's bullying behaviour because she didn't want to make something out of nothing. And she so hoped it was nothing.

By the time Maggie left, she was determined to unravel the mystery of her own family roots. She now understood why she had always loved to bake. If her grandmother was known in Quebec and beyond for her delicate pastries under her Tavie Bakery brand, perhaps Maggie could make a name for herself as well.

She also realized that there had to be a darn good reason for her own mother to lie about her grandmother dying years before Maggie was born. Her family tree seemed to have more twisted branches growing than she'd ever known, and she was determined to solve the mystery.

***

Business at the Cozy Corner Café was brisk, and when Daphne brought Maggie the phone just after lunch, she took it, grateful for the smallest break. She wandered into her office for a bit of quiet, away from the noisy group of tourists at the front tables, laughing and joking over their lunch.

"Hello?" She closed the door part way and leaned against her desk.

"Cousin!" came the booming voice of Francois. "How is your day?"

Maggie's heart dropped. "Francois." This was the last thing she wanted to deal with right now. She stared at the floor, waiting for him to continue.

"Notary Bouchard said it would take some time to sort things out, but I am asking you as my cousin to allow some of my funds to be released to me."

Her shoulders slumped, and she took a deep breath. "I have no control over that. The law is the law, and steps have to be followed. If I could, I would, but it's out of my hands."

The silence on the phone sent a trail of goosebumps down her arms. She heard his ragged breathing for a moment, and then nothing. "I don't believe you are who you say you are," his voice came back, harsh and angry. "I will take this to court and demand that you prove who you are. This should *all* be mine."

"Do whatever you have to do." Maggie wiped a hand on her jeans, a film of sweat having broken out all over her body at his threatening tone.

"It's going to cost you a lot of money." His words sounded chopped, as if each one popping into his head at that exact moment, without any thought of what he was saying. "You'll lose time at the café, and it will get quite messy. Everyone will know your business."

"We'll see." She struggled to keep her words calm.

"You'll regret this," he growled at her.

Maggie jerked as if hit. "Are you threatening me?"

The phone clicked, and the dial tone buzzed in her ear.

Chapter Six

Maggie raced through the woods to Ellie's house minutes later. Not having the kind of phone she could slam down in anger, the childish act of kicking the gravel in her parking lot had not satisfied her at all. How dare this stranger threaten her, and how dare she let his words affect her so much. She shook her head, trying to shake off the fear that had crept in.

Maggie found Ellie and Quinn rocking on the porch swing, Quinn's arm around Ellie's shoulders, both looking quite content.

"Hey there!" Ellie stood to greet her friend with a hug. She pulled back when she felt Maggie shiver. "What's wrong?"

Quinn nodded hello and took another sip of his Coke, watching Maggie's flustered face as Ellie pulled her down onto the steps beside her.

"I need to see what my grandmother left me." Maggie said.

"Good idea." Ellie made a "go on" motion with her hands.

"I know there's a farmhouse and the bakery in town, and I should find out what might need fixing."

"You mean now that Francois isn't taking care of things for your grandmother?"

"He just called and demanded money and swore I'd regret it if I didn't give him something."

Quinn slammed his foot into the porch and sat forward. "He threatened you?"

"That's what it sounded like to me, but I have no proof." Maggie shuddered, as if reliving the exchange with Francois. "But I need to see with my own eyes what is mine, and I guess I have to put my stamp on it."

"What did he say, exactly?" Ellie asked.

"He said he would sue me and make me prove who I am in court."

"You have the documents so..."

"Not all of them." Maggie sat back. "Just *my* birth certificate. I went to see Dad today, and he's going to find their marriage certificate and Mom's birth certificate. But remember, Mom's last name is the same as my grandmother's last name."

Quinn looked from one woman to the other, not quite understanding what that comment meant.

"Yeah," Ellie nodded. "That could be interesting."

"Or difficult?"

"What am I missing?" Quinn asked.

Ellie turned to him. "Most women in Quebec keep their maiden names on all legal documents, and it goes way back. It's the Napoleonic legal system. So, Maggie's mother should have her father's last name, not her mother's."

"Which means?" Quinn asked.

"Which means we don't have Maggie's grandfather's name."

"Will that cause problems?"

"I doubt it." Ellie shook her head. "Just another mystery to solve."

"So, while Dad is looking for the documents," Maggie said, "I'd like to go to St. Anne de Lafont for a couple of days. If you can, we'll go tomorrow. I'll leave Daphne in charge."

"Oh, a road trip!" Ellie clapped her hands together like a child at Christmas.

"That answers that question." Maggie smiled. "It's short notice but..."

"I can be packed in an hour!" Ellie turned to Quinn.

"Yes, yes, I'll take care of Cali, and see if I can't finish the project while you're gallivanting around the province."

"So, what *are* you working on now?" Maggie asked him.

"My last client loved the kitchen set so much that now they want a bedroom ensemble. Old-fashioned; lots of pieces."

"He is talented," Ellie said. "He'll be outgrowing the barn before you know it."

"Not anytime soon, sweetheart." Quinn leaned in and gave her a quick kiss. "I'm enjoying the pace and the perks."

"I bet you are!" Maggie laughed as she stood up. "I'll see you later at the genealogy meeting." She stopped. "You *are* meeting tonight, right?"

Ellie nodded. "Oh, yes, we're talking about wills this time."

"What an appropriate subject," Maggie said.

Ellie wrapped an arm around Quinn's and leaned her head against his shoulder. "You don't mind me leaving like this?"

"Not at all." He pulled her close. "I'll have plenty to do, and my furry friend will keep me company. And now it's back to work." He headed for the barn, Cali at his side.

"As if doing something you love could ever be work!" Ellie said.

He turned, but continued walking backwards. "Then aren't we both the lucky ones?"

"You're such a mushy couple." Maggie laughed as she entered the woods. "I love it!" she called over her shoulder as she disappeared.

***

The Café had only a few customers when Ellie arrived that evening, but the chatter from the back room, where her Genealogy Seniors group was meeting, made her smile. They had been meeting for almost a year and, as a team, they had solved a few mysteries, as well as learned how to write their own personal histories. They were people who had come together and become friends.

Maggie came out of the kitchen and took her arm. "Is seven o'clock too early for you tomorrow? I want as much time as possible to explore everything at my grandmother's."

Ellie loved Maggie's excitement and gave her a quick hug. "I can't wait to go! I finished the first draft of the book and need to put it aside for a while. Seven o'clock is perfect."

"I'll pick you up." Maggie went to prepare the snack she always provided for the meeting.

The seniors turned to Ellie as she entered the book-lined room at the back of the Café. A meeting place, a reading retreat, and more, the Café had become a focal point for both passing tourists and residents of Percyville.

"You'll never guess what an artist our Phil is!" Lennie said from his seat beside his wife Tess. "Look at the floor plan he drew of his childhood home."

"Lennie!" His wife, Tess, shook her head at him, warning him not to tease Phil.

"No, really," Lennie said, "he's got a knack for it."

Ellie noticed the various pieces of paper scattered across the table; some being passed around for everyone to see. Lennie held up Phil's, and Ellie took it from him as she her briefcase on the chair in front of her. "My goodness, Phil." She peeked over the top of the paper at Phil to see his face turning red from all the attention. "This is quite something!"

"Thank you." It had taken a few months for Phil to come out of his shell, but being dragged to the meetings by his friend Ruth had done wonders for the widower. "I had forgotten a few things before I tried this exercise. We had the most wonderful porch out back, all screened in for the summer. My brother and I would sleep out there on the hottest days. And I'll admit, I'd be the one to run inside when the animals started making noises in the dark."

"That must have been fun!" Ellie's Aunt Norma said from her seat next to Phil. She had taken a liking to Phil from the moment she had joined the group the previous month, but Phil had seemed oblivious to her overtures. But with her quirky clothes and ever-present smile, Norma had been accepted into the group and was enjoying the company more than she expected.

"You've all done an amazing job." Ellie sat down and took the floor plan of her own childhood out of her bag and passed it around. "Has anyone found anything interesting?"

They all knew what she meant. Interesting to Ellie meant out of the ordinary and sometimes scandalous. She liked to remind them that the past often held secrets.

"Actually," Doreen Hastings said from across the table, "I drew the first house I lived in when I got married." They all knew what a terrible time Doreen had gone through when her husband and best friend of sixty-five years had died a few years earlier. She had healed with the help of her friends and family, but without her husband, she had floundered for the first year. "I remember thinking how big this place was and worrying that we'd never be able to fill it with our few pieces. Little did I know we'd soon be moving to make room for the kids." She looked at the paper in her hands. "Funny how one day's worries turn out to be the joys of the next."

"Ellie, this is the house your father grew up in." Norma handed her a piece of paper with the most lopsided house Ellie had ever seen. Each room was labeled and she squinted to see the room her father had grown up in.

"That's a very small room," Ellie said.

"Oh, nonsense," Norma laughed. "It's definitely not to scale, but his room was smaller because he was the only boy and had to have his own room. The trouble was, we girls loved to use it for fort building!"

"I never knew that," Ellie said.

"I didn't remember it until this assignment, to be honest."

Ellie looked around at her friends and caught Ruth's eye. Ruth was sitting next to Shirley, the two of them whispering over a drawing. "And what have you brought us, Ruth?" Ruth had always been her favorite of the sisters. She was a retired popular schoolteacher, and considered by most to be everyone's grandmother in the community, a source of knowledge and wisdom on many subjects.

"Well." Ruth turned to her sister, who nodded for her to continue. "Since Shirley and I have always lived together, we chose the farmhouse, of course."

Ellie craned her neck to see the paper, and Ruth handed it to her. Noting the gentle lines of her current home, Ellie frowned and put her finger on a particular room at the back of the second floor. "What is this? I've never seen this before."

Ruth and Shirley shared a glance and then Shirley, usually the more outgoing and vocal of the two, answered quietly. "It was our playroom. We got there by crawling through a little door that Dad cut through the wall of our bedroom, through the closet actually."

"I'm so sorry, Ellie." Ruth seemed quite concerned. "We forgot all about it until we drew the plan, so we couldn't have told you about it when you bought the house from us."

Ellie leaned back in her seat and smiled. "Winnie would have loved this room."

The group looked from one to the other, not sure if the subject of her late daughter and husband was now open for discussion. The years had passed, and they'd all watched Ellie's slow recovery, but this was the first time she'd spoken about her family since these meetings began.

"Yes, well," Shirley blustered. "I hated the cobwebs and spiders, and all we had for light was a flashlight." She shuddered.

"I loved it!" Ruth said. "It was the perfect girl cave."

"I'll definitely look for it later." Ellie handed the drawing back.

"And what lesson are you going to teach us today?" Tess reached for her husband's hand and squeezed it excitedly. Tess the social one; Lennie the grumpy one. An ideal match.

"I thought we'd talk about wills." Ellie took a copy of her own will from her bag. "Whether you've ever received an inheritance, whether you have a will, and if not, why, for goodness' sake you don't."

Maggie came to the table and placed a plate of cookies in the middle, while Daphne followed with a tray of teacups and accessories. "I'd love to sit in on this."

Maggie took an empty seat beside Phil. They were surprised she was joining them, but welcomed her to the table.

"Can I use your story?" Ellie asked her. The group perked up with interest.

"Sure," Maggie said. "Maybe I'll learn something."

Lennie spoke first. "Everyone here knows I was a lawyer, and I have experience with wills, so if there are any questions afterwards, I'll be happy to answer them."

"Oh, there might be," Maggie assured him with a nod, folding her arms on the table and waiting for Ellie to begin.

"Where there's a will, there's a way," Doreen Hastings quipped, her needles clicking away as she knitted. Ellie figured Doreen was making another scarf, which appeared to be the only thing Doreen ever made, but the older woman enjoyed keeping her fingers busy.

"Lennie, can you prepare your own will?" Phil asked, pen in hand above a pad, ready to take notes.

"You certainly can," Lennie said. "But you have to follow certain guidelines. I'd still advise you to do it with a professional. A notarized will can make it a lot easier for your executor to settle your estate. Especially if your executor is a family member. They'll be grieving for your passing, but making the whole process as easy as possible is the ultimate gift you can give them."

They all sat still, and when Lennie realized they were waiting for him to continue, he sat up straighter and looked at Ellie.

"Please, Lennie, if you have any nuggets of information, do share them," she said.

"Well, at this point in our lives..." He scanned the faces of his fellow seniors. "I'm sure we know who we want to leave things to. You might have specific items you want certain people to get, and you can put that in your will. And you don't have to leave anything to anyone you don't want to, even if you once said you would. Also, if you can list your assets, that would be good too."

"Before we go any further," Ellie said, "who has a will?" She watched as they all raised their hands, except for Norma.

"I never got around to it," she shrugged her shoulders, as if the idea had never occurred to her.

"I think it would make life easier for your children," Lennie said. "It's just one less thing for them to worry about when you..."

"When I kick the bucket?" Norma asked.

Phil snorted, then tried to hide it with a cough. He took a side glance at her and she winked at him.

"I made one years ago," Ruth said. "I'm not sure it's any good though."

Lennie nodded. "If it goes through a notary and is recorded, it's still good."

"We should redo ours, dear," Tess told him. "Now that we have great-grandchildren, we should make some special bequests for them."

"And who has changed their wills in the last five to ten years?" Ellie asked.

Doreen was the only one to raise her hand. "My kids suggested that I do it last year. I originally left everything to my husband, and he left everything to me. After that, we left it to Richard, our son, and we used some phrase like any other offspring that comes from this marriage."

"Good idea to update that," Lennie agreed.

"The reason I'm asking if you've changed it is because our circumstances change over the years," Ellie said. "For example, you should probably remove any item about guardians for your children."

They all laughed, knowing that some day those same children might become *their* guardians.

"Or change the executor of your estate," Ellie continued. "Although I must admit, I *have* found a lot of interesting things in wills. Like children no one knew about, children who weren't even mentioned, in-laws taking precedence over one's own child, previous marriages, mistresses acknowledged with gifts."

"We're keeping it simple," Shirley said. "Ruth and I are leaving everything for each other."

"And when the last one of you dies, who gets your estate?" Phil asked.

"We'd rather not discuss that," Shirley said.

Phil nodded, acknowledging her privacy.

"What I'd like you to do," Ellie continued, leaning forward on the table, "is to review your wills. Make sure you've listed all your assets. You may have purchased new items since you first had the will drawn up. Make sure the wording reflects your current wishes. A little updating wouldn't hurt, or it could be perfect the way it is. And those of you without a will," she looked directly at her aunt, "really need to get a move on."

Norma nodded her agreement.

"And if you need advice," Tess piped in, "Lennie will be happy to answer your questions."

Lennie nodded. "Sure, no problem. Could be fun." He said the last part as if trying to convince himself that he hadn't let himself in for something unpleasant.

"And what's Maggie's part in all this?" Ruth asked, tapping her fingers on the table, impatient to get to the heart of the lesson.

Ellie sat back and made herself comfortable. "Maggie came into an inheritance."

"From a grandmother I didn't know was still alive!" Maggie blurted out.

For the next few minutes Ellie explained Maggie's situation, with Maggie throwing in a few words about Francois and his behavior.

"Oh, heavens!" Tess said. "He's threatening you?"

"He doesn't have a leg to stand on," Lennie assured her.

"But what if I can't prove who I am?" Maggie asked. "What if my mother was illegitimate, which I'm beginning to suspect, and I have got no documentary proof linking her to my grandmother?"

"Notary Bouchard seems to think there's nothing wrong," Lennie said.

"Yes, but Francois said he'd sue me because I have no tangible connection to my grandmother." Maggie said. "He wants me to prove who I am."

"He's bluffing," Lennie assured her. "Anyone can leave their estate, or parts thereof, to anyone they wish. It does *not* have to be a family member."

"Anybody ever inherit anything interesting?" Phil looked around at his friends, trying to lighten the mood.

"Have you?" Doreen asked him.

"I have." He pulled out his wallet and took a picture from inside. "When I was about twenty-five, my grandfather left me this car." He passed it around and smiled at the oohs and aahs. "He saw it in England, and had one shipped home."

"That must have cost a fortune," Lennie said, eyeing the car and nodding his approval.

"My grandfather had a lot of money, for a short time, and spent it all. The rest of the family had to work very hard to get by." Phil shook his head. "Life was different then."

"And where is it now?" Shirley asked him, quite liking the two-seater MG TC Midget.

"I sold it for a down payment on my first house," he sighed, as if the memories were well worth it. "It was the car of my youth, and I never enjoyed another one quite as much."

Norma turned to Maggie. "So, what did your grandmother leave you?"

Maggie hesitated, but when she saw the group of eager faces before her, she jumped right in. "She left me her home in St. Anne de Lafont and the Tavie Bakery."

As everyone's mouths dropped open in surprise, Maggie headed back to work, feeling like she was on stronger ground with Lenny's assurances ringing in her ears.

"I knew Maggie had a gift for baking," Tess said. "And now we know why!"

Chapter Seven

A thin veil of mist covered the land as Maggie arrived at seven sharp to pick up Ellie for their trip. It slid across the fields, wrapped around the trees, then slowly disappeared as the sun rose higher.

Ellie's bag was by the front door when Maggie arrived. She watched Ellie and Cali emerge from the forest just as Quinn stepped out from the barn at the sound of her car. He greeted Maggie with a hearty good morning, and stowed Ellie's luggage in the back seat.

Maggie jumped from the car as Ellie reached her and hugged her so tight that she lifted Ellie off the ground. "I am so excited!"

"I can tell," Ellie laughed.

"Sorry!" Maggie put her down and stepped back. "Is it okay to be terrified at the same time?"

"Of course," Ellie said. "This is a big event in anyone's life, and I bet you're going to feel a whole range of emotions before it's over."

Quinn enveloped Ellie in his arms from behind, resting his chin on the top of her head. "You ladies have fun on your adventure." He turned Ellie around and gave her a quick but deep kiss. "I almost envy you."

"Ha!" Ellie swatted him playfully. "There's nothing you'd hate more than a road trip. But I can't wait to see the headboard you're making when I get back."

He bowed to her. "Of course, milady."

Maggie stared at him in astonishment. "Does she have you watching Downton Abbey?"

"I sit by her side while she binges, but..." He shrugged in defeat.

"Baloney." Ellie grinned. "He loves it as much as I do." She leaned down to give Cali some last-minute love, then strode to the car. "You two behave yourselves while I'm gone."

Quinn looked at Cali and the dog returned his glance, as if she understood the conversation and knew they would ignore it. "Late nights and overeating for both of us," Quinn said.

From behind the wheel, Maggie watched as Ellie ran back to him for one last kiss and hug before climbing into the passenger seat. "Ta, ta, all!" Ellie called from the car as they drove down the driveway.

***

Leaving early, they beat the work traffic and school buses in their area, and were on the secondary highway in less than an hour. They took a longer route, enjoying the back roads of Quebec as it gave them time to chat and relax. Maggie had provided some of her delicious pastries, but they stopped at a Tim Horton's drive-through for Ellie's favorite coffee, a Caramel Macchiato. Maggie preferred a cup of tea.

After they had devoured the croissants, Ellie gathered the napkins and empty cups into a garbage bag, then leaned back in her seat. "How do you feel about this?" She glanced at Maggie and caught her friend's jaw clench at the question.

"I tossed and turned all night," Maggie said as she put on her turn signal to pass a slow-moving car. "I was angry at first, but I'm not sure who with. My mom for not telling me my grandmother was still alive? Or at my grandmother for never acknowledging me?"

"There must be a reason."

"What would keep someone from visiting their grandchild?"

Ellie had no answer for her.

"I mean, did she hate me?" Maggie continued.

"Who?"

"Either of them." Maggie let out a breath of frustration. "Then I spent a good hour wondering what Mom might have done to make her own mother disown her."

"Or..."

"Perhaps it was the other way around." Maggie pulled into the slower lane.

"Maybe we'll find the answer at your grandmother's house."

"And how are you and Quinn doing?" Maggie turned the conversation to Ellie's personal life. "You *were* pretty smoochy back there."

Ellie stared at her friend, eyes narrowed, a grin on her lips. "We're fine, thanks for asking, *again.* And how are you and Pete?" Two could play at this game.

Maggie laughed out loud. "Do you realize that we've been best friends for years, yet we rarely talk about the actual details of our personal relationships?"

"You mean the men in our lives?" Ellie turned away, hiding a frown at the fleeting memory of her late husband and daughter. The pain of their loss had lessened over the years, but the memories remained clear. Now she was working on the guilt of moving on with her life. "For me it was just Adam, and you were married to your business! But we *were* pretty flippant about it. Maybe that's why we keep asking now. Hoping that something has changed for us."

"I never thought you'd date again," Maggie confessed. "And here you are, letting a stranger stay in your house. And kiss you goodnight! So, yeah, something's changed."

"The way Quinn and I were thrown together, you get to know someone fast," Ellie admitted. "I enjoy having him around. He calms me down. He's a good man, and I trust my gut."

"And?" Maggie glanced at her, waiting for the response she knew would come.

"And he's a great kisser!"

"But you're still going slow?"

Ellie hesitated, not sure how to answer the question, not even how to answer it for herself. The attraction between Quinn and her had been like an explosion, one they'd both been suspicious of at first. As the weeks passed and they'd spent time together, Quinn renting her barn to set up his furniture business, and her allowing him to rent a room in her farmhouse, they'd grown to appreciate each other. The kisses were the icing on the cake. It was as if they had no choice, the attraction was so strong.

"I think we're both afraid of this," Ellie said.

Maggie was silent for a minute. "I've never heard you say you were afraid of anything before."

"Don't let this happy face fool you. I think Quinn and I want to be sure of each other and our feelings before jumping into a physical relationship." Ellie turned her attention to the fields outside her window as they drove through another farm town. "We want to be friends first, if that makes any sense."

"Totally makes sense," Maggie said. "Pete and I felt the same at first, but..."

"Oh, you've made a fallen man out of him, have you?" Ellie joked.

"We fell together, and I've never been happier."

They drove for another hour listening to music, enjoying the morning sun, lost in their own thoughts. Maggie slowed down when they reached the bridge that would take them across the small river to St. Anne de Lafont, the town where her grandmother had lived. "What's this?"

A police car blocked traffic while an officer directed people to turn around. As they approached the front of the line, Maggie rolled down her window. "Excuse me, how long is this going to be closed?"

The young officer leaned in towards her. "They're trying to hoist a sheep that fell into the river. It's stuck on the rocks." Although his badge read Tremblay, Maggie and Ellie were relieved to find his English was good. He glanced back across the bridge. "It could be a couple of hours."

"But I need to get to St. Anne de Lafont." The strain of having to find another route caught in Maggie's voice as she pointed to the outline of the town beyond the woods.

"You can turn around and head back to the highway, head east for about fifty kilometers until you get to Carnac, and get into town that way."

Ellie leaned over and got his attention. "You mean this is the only way to get to St. Anne de Lafont from this direction?"

He shrugged. "Sorry. It's the main entrance. There was talk of building another bridge years ago, but..." He shrugged again and walked away, motioning for the car behind them to turn around.

Maggie pulled off the road, still facing the bridge. "What should we do?"

Ellie opened her door and got out. "I've never seen a sheep hoisted out of a river before, have you?"

Chapter Eight

The expected delay of a few hours ended up being only forty-five minutes, and before they knew it, they were crossing the wooden bridge behind a farmer's truck with a wet sheep's head sticking out the back. The thump, thump of the bridge's planks filled the car as they crossed and hit the dirt road beyond.

A church steeple was the tallest structure in the distance, adding a fairy tale quality to their adventure. Through the woods they caught glimpses of farmhouses, and as they left the wooded area, they entered the town itself. The church welcomed them on their left, with a peaceful cemetery behind it Old homes, some renovated and turned into mom-and-pop shops, lined the road, while a large green space occupied the middle of Rue Principale. A side street led around the church, large oak trees filling the green space, with benches placed in the shade of each one.

They drove slowly, Ellie checking the handwritten directions Notary Bouchard had provided. "There!" Ellie pointed. They stopped on the other side of the church to check the street name. "Rue St. Anne. This is it."

Maggie hesitated; her eyes drawn to a business sign at the end of a cluster of shops along the main street. Boulangerie Tavie Bakery. It was bright red, and someone had delicately painted the image of an older woman on it. She recognized it from the Tavie Bakery pastry container she had finished before leaving home that morning, now sitting empty on her counter.

Ellie followed her gaze. "Now or later?"

Maggie stepped on the gas and headed down Rue St. Anne. "Later. I need to see my grandmother's house before I go to the bakery. I want to ground myself a bit."

Following the directions once again, they drove down Rue St. Anne until they reached Octavie's single-lane dirt driveway. The branches of the trees on either side met across the road to form a green tunnel, and the sun barely filtered through. Maggie slowed down as they both looked out at the sight before them.

They left the canopy of trees, and the driveway opened onto an expansive lawn.

"Oh, my," Ellie whispered. Maggie stopped the car abruptly.

Mature and majestic oaks surrounded an old farmhouse, shading it from the morning sun. They sat for a moment, taking it all in, before Maggie slipped out and grabbed the car door and roof for support. Ellie followed.

"I wasn't expecting anything so..." Maggie's voice trailed off, at a loss for words.

"So perfect?" Ellie headed to the house, glancing around in wonder, trying to see everything at once. The farmhouse itself sat on the highest point, with a rolling lawn to the left where it met a dense forest. Between the house and the woods, surrounded by a sturdy chain-link fence, was a lush vegetable garden. To the right was a large barn, its doors secured by a heavy lock. Beyond that, they could make out a grove of apple trees occupying a fair amount of land.

Climbing the stairs, they reached the balcony together and walked its length, then around a corner. As they came to the back of the house, they heard a creek meandering past at the bottom of the open field. In the distance they saw a wooden bridge that crossed over.

"Oh, my," Maggie said, shaking her head in amazement.

"And this is just the outside!" Ellie laughed, pleased that her friend had inherited this wonderland. "Where to start?"

Maggie pulled her eyes away from the creek, and the possibilities of what lay beyond it, and studied the house itself. "How about we check out the grounds first?"

Ellie leaned close to a window and cupped her hands to peer inside. "Oh, look, there's one of those old roll-top desks!"

The sound of a loud engine in the morning's silence alerted them to a visitor heading their way. A red pickup truck barreled up the road, squealing to a stop behind Maggie's car. To their dismay, out climbed Francois and a young woman, both dressed in dirty jeans and t-shirts, as if they had spent the morning cleaning someone's garage.

He strolled over with a big smile on his face. "I thought I'd get here before you."

"I don't remember us scheduling a meeting," Maggie replied stiffly.

"Well, no." He shook his head. His girlfriend gave him the side-eye, hands in her pockets, avoiding any direct interaction with Maggie and Ellie. "But I need to explain how things work around here. I have a lot of work to do."

"I think we can handle it all on our own," Maggie said.

"No, no!" Francois insisted. "You don't understand. There are ongoing daily matters that need to be taken care of."

Maggie gave him a look. He had the grace to look away, directly into the eyes of his girlfriend, who gave him a silent nudge with a jerk of her head.

"Like I said," Maggie repeated, "we'll be fine."

"But here's the thing." Francois gave her a sheepish smile, and spread his arms wide. "There's so much to deal with here. If you let me take it off your hands, I'll make sure it's all taken care of."

"You want her to *give* it to you?" Ellie asked, her eyes wide in surprise.

"I don't think you have the money to buy it," Maggie said. Her head tilted to one side as she stared at his face, as if trying to get the real measure of him. "And if I wanted to sell, I'd sell it to someone at a fair market value. Can you afford that?"

"Well..." he stumbled.

"So, that's it then." Maggie moved forward, crowding into his space, and Ellie followed close behind. "There's no need for you to come back."

"But the work," he sputtered.

"If anything needs doing, I'll find someone."

"You're a nasty piece of..." Francois's girlfriend said before he raised his hand to stop her, but she refused to be silenced. "He's worked hard for this property all these years."

Maggie turned her full attention to the young woman. "If he did, I'm sure my grandmother paid him for his work."

The silence that followed became a battle of wills. No one moved.

Ellie clapped her hands together, and everyone jumped. "That's it, goodbye." She walked away, giving Maggie a quick nod for her to follow. Which she did.

They made it to the barn before they heard the squeal of Francois's retreating truck tires and blare of his horn, long and unrepentant, as if his finger was glued to the button.

***

Maggie leaned against the rough wood of the peeling barn and pressed a hand to her chest. "He's so..."

"Scary?" Ellie asked. She peered around the corner and watched the dust settle on the road.

"More like creepy and overwhelming." Maggie shook her head as she looked out at the orchard. "I can't believe all this is mine. No wonder he wants it."

Ellie grabbed her arm. "Let's go check it out. Do you have the property map?"

Maggie pulled out an old certificate of location. "Here." She unfolded it and tapped the document in a couple of places. "Is this the creek? And what do you think that building is?"

Ellie studied the map, then looked over the land, her eyes sweeping from side to side, then back to the map. She pointed ahead of them. "That's the creek here." She poked the map and kept her finger on it, pointing and looking at the surrounding land. "And over there..." With her other hand, she pointed across the vegetable garden and beyond. "That's another building there."

"And this?" Maggie pointed to a structure that crossed the water. "The bridge?"

"An adventure!" Ellie grinned at her and headed off in that direction.

"It's like a fairy tale," Maggie called from behind her.

"With no evil witches."

"But a creepy cousin." Maggie managed a laugh. Ellie was glad to see Maggie recovering from her cousin's intrusion.

They meandered along the path around the garden, through the sun-drenched field to the edge of the creek. The bottom was filled with rocks they could use to step across. Even though the bank was only twenty feet away, they turned left, following what appeared to be an animal trail leading to the small bridge.

Maggie eyed the wooden structure and gave the railing a vigorous shake. "It seems strong enough to..."

Ellie had breezed past her and was already on the other side, waiting for her. "Catch up slow poke, the cabin is just beyond that grove of trees." She pointed to a path that disappeared behind a stand of cedars that camouflaged the building beyond. Maggie followed her lead, and when they reached the bend in the path, they both stopped in astonishment.

A miniature version of the main house lay before them. One story, a large porch, windows flanking the front door, and a rocking chair resting under the overhang.

The sound of a wind chime echoed as a gentle breeze blew through the trees.

They approached the building reverently, as if they knew that this was a special place for Octavie. The windows shone in the sun as if someone had washed them that morning, and white curtains with a carnation print covered them both. The land around the cabin was cleared to about ten feet, almost within the reach of a tall man who spread his arms wide as he walked the perimeter; the house on one side, sheltering trees on the other.

Maggie stepped onto the porch and reached for the doorknob, stopping when confronted with a brand-new lock. She turned to Ellie in disappointment. "I don't think we can get in."

Ellie peered through a window and saw a double bed with a faded green quilt. "I bet one of those keys Notary Bouchard gave you on that big keyring is for this door." She laughed and held out her hand. "Give me the keys and I'll give it a try."

Maggie hesitated before dropping the clinking bundle into Ellie's hands. "I'll go around back and check things out."

Ellie made a shooing motion. "Off you go, Lady Marguerite. The castle awaits, and you must view your new kingdom."

With the sound of keys being inserted in the lock, Maggie continued around the side of the building.

***

The porch stretched only across the front of the cabin. Maggie strolled along the side of the building, wood chips at her feet, the forest just a touch away. A single window filled the side wall, and within seconds she found herself at the back. The land opened up, and a path led from a set of old wooden stairs, all in good repair but weathered. At the side of the stairs was a stacked pile of wood, protected by a tarp. Enough for a long, cold Quebec winter.

A tartan hammock was slung between two large oak trees, low enough for an elderly woman to get in and out of with ease. Maggie picked up a walking stick that rested against one of the trunks, its head worn smooth from use.

The path wound around some bushes and large boulders and ended at a quaint outhouse, the half-moon cut-out on the door covered with a fine screen. Beyond the building, the forest encircled everything, the lowest branches of many trees so high that one could easily walk under them unimpeded. Pine needles and leaves littered the ground, and all she could see, in any direction, were more trees.

Maggie pulled out the map again and located the cabin and outhouse on it. According to the document, she now owned at least twenty acres back from the cabin. The map showed various features of the property, the buildings, the creek, the road, and some handwritten notes she couldn't quite make out. The main house and this tiny cabin were in the middle of the property, surrounded by forest. She had no idea how close the nearest neighbor was, but as she paused beside the outhouse, she heard nothing but the birds flying through the branches of the trees, calling to each other.

When Maggie returned to the porch, she found Ellie sitting on the steps, tossing the keys from one hand to the other. "No luck?" she asked

Ellie shook her head. "Nope. We're going to need a crowbar or something to get this lock off. What's that?" She pointed to the walking stick Maggie was carrying.

"I found it near a hammock out back." She held it tight. "It was probably my grandmother's." Maggie held out her hand and helped Ellie to her feet. "We'll come back later. Let's check out the farmhouse. But if you need to use the facilities, there's a lovely outhouse in the rear."

"I hope the main house has an indoor toilet."

The women chuckled as they made their way back over the bridge and through the field.

Chapter Nine

When they arrived at the house, Ellie peered through every window she could reach, trying to see the lay of the rooms beyond.

Maggie grabbed her sleeve and pulled her to the front door. "We can go in. No need to be a peeping tom." She held out her hand for the keys and Ellie dropped them into her palm. She found one with a tag marked "Main House". It was a new key, still shiny, as if seldom used. "I guess we know why she changed the locks." She opened the screen door and unlocked the wooden front door before stepping through, waiting for Ellie to follow.

They were in an entryway, a bench to one side and a row of hooks along the opposite wall. A worn red plaid jacket hung from one, and a green plaid hat rested beside it. Bright blue rubber boots were tucked under the bench, and a pair of yellow crocs sat in the doorway to the house. Their reflections in the mirror on the wall showed their windblown hair, rosy faces, and eyes full of wonder.

"It's like Christmas," Maggie whispered. "I'm about to walk into a huge present and I have no idea what to expect."

"Why are you whispering?"

Maggie turned in surprise. "I have no idea, but it seems wrong to be walking into the house of someone I've never met."

"She left it to you because she wanted you to have it." Ellie pushed her forward. "I'm so curious about her."

They took off their shoes and stepped into the living room, feeling the worn wooden floorboards beneath their stocking feet. The farmhouse itself had an open floor plan. A living room, with a stone fireplace, surrounded by a couch and chair that led to a small dining area with a rustic table and four seats. On the other side of the ground floor was a wraparound kitchen with an island counter that created a simple separation. To the right, they found a powder room, with a staircase leading up. Taking a step further into the room, Maggie found a small pantry behind the stairs, its shelves half full of homemade preserves. Each glass jar contained a handwritten label identifying the contents.

Ellie wandered around the living room, glancing at the artwork on the walls and stopping at the mantle above the fireplace. "Look at this."

Maggie joined her. Ellie was holding a picture. It was of Maggie, age five, heading off to school. There were other photos alongside it. In a delicate gold frame, was a picture of Maggie's graduation; next to it was a picture of Maggie at the opening of the Cozy Corner Café. In each picture, she was beaming, proud of herself for each accomplishment, at each age. "Where did she get all these?"

"Maybe your mother was still in touch with your grandmother?"

Maggie took the picture of her five-year-old self from Ellie and sighed. "I would have loved to have had a grandmother, Ellie. All my friends did. Why would Mom do that?"

"Let's look around. There might be something here that explains it all," Ellie said, moving away from the gallery of pictures.

"I'm hungry," Maggie said.

"You mean borderline hangry?" Ellie joked.

"Almost there." Maggie opened the fridge, expecting to find empty shelves, but instead was startled to find it half stocked. "What the...?"

Ellie peered inside and smiled. "Maybe we don't need the food we brought after all." She reached in and pulled out a meat pie. "We've got supper here, but how about we eat our own sandwiches for lunch?"

"And then we'll check out the grounds while we have good light. We can finish up in here later."

***

Since it was tick season, they changed into long pants and running shoes with high socks to cover their ankles and legs as they trudged through the woods. The quick tour they had taken earlier would be nothing compared to this trip.

Ellie plopped down on the top step of the porch and pulled out the certificate of location and studied it closely.

"Look at this." She waited for Maggie to sit beside her, and then pointed out some handwritten notes. "Someone took the time to show off the land."

Maggie tapped the paper at the far end of the creek. "What's this? I can't read it."

Ellie squinted at the spot. "I think it says hammock."

"Another one? Fun!"

"So, how do we do this? Work our way along the survey lines, popping in and out when we find something interesting?"

Maggie nodded. "Sounds like a plan. These notes must have some special meaning if someone left them here. I want to find every nook and cranny."

"That'll take a while."

Maggie got up and headed inside. "Then I'll get us some water bottles and a snack."

When she returned moments later, she had a small backpack on her back and her key ring jingling in her hand. She tossed a hat to Ellie and pulled her Montreal Canadiens cap firmly on, before locking the front door tight.

"How about we go to the end of the driveway and walk along the road until we reach the line and work from there?" Ellie suggested.

"Let's go."

The sun scorched the tops of their heads and they were grateful for the hats by the time they made it to the road. They turned left, away from town, and it took nearly fifteen minutes to reach the boundary marker indicated on the map. A low rock wall separated Maggie's property from the field on the other side, but the unspoiled forest of trees compared to the open cultivated field was an even clearer sign of the boundary.

Maggie ran her fingers across the rocks. "This is pretty cool."

"This is how farmers used to do things. It's not a fancy fence, just enough to keep cattle from crossing and to make sure there was no dispute about whose land was whose."

They continued along the inside of the rock boundary, appreciating the shade of the trees above. "Listen to that!" Maggie tilted her head back to watch the flock of small birds flying from tree to tree, chattering at them with all their might.

"Maybe we're in their neighborhood." Ellie followed the activity above. "I doubt they get many people out here."

"Is there anything interesting to see in this area?"

Ellie pulled out the map, and they both studied it. She ran her finger along the line of the boundary wall and stopped at a treehouse marked with an X. "This could be interesting."

"Lead the way." Maggie hoisted the pack higher on her back and followed Ellie between the trees, away from the boundary line and deeper into the forest.

Another five minutes of walking along an animal trail brought them to the base of two massive Tamaracks. An ancient wooden ladder snaked up the side of one trunk to a small structure above.

"Remind you of anything?" Maggie asked.

"It looks a little like the one Ruth and Shirley's dad built. I guess it was something they did back then, because I haven't seen many new treehouses these days."

Maggie shook the ladder hard, then shook it again and nodded. "It's good. You ready for this?"

"After you." Ellie watched as her friend scampered up the rungs, pushed open the trapdoor, and disappeared inside.

Maggie's head reappeared through the hole. "Get up here, quick!"

Ellie followed more slowly, testing each rung as she climbed. Heights were not her thing, but mysteries were. She reached the top and stopped dead when her shoulders cleared the floorboards.

"Check this out!" Maggie flopped onto a pile of colorful cushions in a space that could fit three people spread out, with room to spare. An old rug covered the floorboards, and a couple of low tables stood between other groupings of cushions. "How hippie-dippy is this!"

Ellie crawled the rest of the way into the treehouse and closed the trapdoor behind her. A six-foot-tall person could stand in the middle, though the sides of the roof sloped to the ground. One window faced south, and the sun tried to beat through the simple floral curtain that hung over it. She drew it back to see the forest beyond, the creek in the distance.

"Isn't this the best?" Maggie giggled like a child discovering the perfect place to begin an adventure.

Ellie sank onto the cushions and took in the small room. "Who do you think made this? I mean, this place is clean, like housekeeping came by an hour ago!"

Maggie controlled her excitement and nodded. "Are you sure this is on my property, not the other one?"

Ellie studied the map again. "Nope, it's yours."

"Look at these drawings." Maggie got down on her knees and crawled around the room, spending time at each drawing that adorned the walls. There were ten in all, and each depicted the farm from different angles.

Ellie pointed to one by her shoulder. "There, in the background, behind the barn. What's that?"

Maggie leaned forward and frowned. "It's a person. A man?"

"With a big beard."

"And he's in this one too," Maggie gestured to another. She turned and studied each drawing.

"He's in all of them, sometimes just a shadow."

"Hmm." Maggie took the pictures off the walls, carefully removing the tacks and stacking them on the floor. "He must have been important to my grandmother."

"Could be another piece of the family puzzle," Ellie said. She handed Maggie the remaining sketches, and watched as Maggie smooth them all out and put them in her backpack.

"I can't have them ruined."

"And the cushions and..." Ellie pointed to the other things in the room.

"Later." Maggie looked at the ceiling. "This place has to be waterproof, but I'm not taking any chances with the drawings. Okay, I'm done here, for now."

Chapter Ten

Back on the ground, they returned to the border wall and followed it to the creek. There was nothing else of interest on the map in this area, but Maggie was curious about the places that were highlighted.

"We're on a treasure hunt!" Ellie said, her arms swinging in the breeze, a big smile on her face.

"I have to admit," Maggie said, letting one arm go for a tentative swing, "I feel like I'm ten again." And before she knew it, both arms were swinging in time with Ellie's and the glitter of the creek in the distance caught their eyes.

They reached the bank and were surprised to see how wide the creek was at this point, twice as wide across as it had been at the cabin, and twice as deep. There was no way to cross it.

The map showed that Maggie owned another twenty acres on the other side. "That'll have to wait for another day," Maggie said. "And there's nothing marked on that side. But here..." She consulted the map and turned around slowly, checking each tree until she found the one highlighted. "There's the second hammock."

Ellie walked over and pulled a canvas sack away from the trunk. "It's a big one." One end was attached to a large bolt. They unwrapped it and looked for a place to hook the other end.

"Here," Maggie touched a spot on a tree ten feet away and reached for the bolt that rested near her head.

After they attached the loose end, the hammock swayed in the breeze. Ellie held out her hand as if to say, "After you", and Maggie tucked the webbing under her behind and legs and leaned back. Ellie climbed on next to her.

"This is nice," Ellie murmured.

They could sit and face the water, or stretch the cloth behind their heads and lean back, which they did. The trees above provided a leafy canopy that allowed trickles of warm sunlight to caress their faces. The creek gurgled as it flowed over rocks and under fallen logs, before disappearing around a bend.

"Snack time," Maggie said as she pulled the backpack onto the hammock and removed the water bottles and energy bars.

They sat in silence, eating and swinging with a gentle push of a toe on the ground. Within minutes of finishing and laying their heads back, they were both dozing in the gentle motion.

When Ellie awoke from her nap, something caught her eye across the creek. A deer was grazing, unaware of the two people lying a short distance away. When Maggie stirred, Ellie put her hand on Maggie's and squeezed, hoping she'd understand to be still. She did.

The deer moved from one patch of grass to another, its head popping up, ears twitching, as if it sensed danger. It retreated, its eyes searching for whatever it was that had disturbed it. It remained frozen for a few seconds, and then it was gone, dashing through the forest and disappearing into the trees.

"Well." Maggie gathered her things. "What a perfect end to our nap."

"I'm surprised your snoring didn't scare it away," Ellie joked as she scrambled out of the hammock and put it back in its protective bag.

"I do *not* snore!" Maggie asserted as they continued down the trail.

"Like an elephant."

***

The next half hour took them back to the bridge near the cabin, but they passed it and ended at a marker several acres away.

Maggie gazed across another field, to a second stone wall that stood between her property and it. "So, my land is a forest surrounded by farms."

Ellie had the map in her hand and checked it quickly. "There's a lot of land past the cabin and across the creek to check out."

"I'm going to save that for another time." Maggie turned back to the bridge and the farmhouse. "But I *am* curious to see what my grandmother grew in her garden."

When they reached the enclosed space, the women stopped in amazement.

"It's huge," Ellie said. "How did she work this whole area?"

"She must have had help."

"Francois?" Ellie spat out the name, then followed it with a shudder.

"He doesn't seem like the gardening type. More like the sit-down mower type."

They fanned out and walked the various paths, calling out the names of the vegetables or fruit they found growing there by the neatly labeled sticks.

"She had this all planted before she died," Ellie murmured.

"Amazing." Maggie bent down to read a label. "So much is ready to harvest already. How am I going to take care of it if I'm so far away?"

"Maybe you can hire someone from around here." Ellie joined her at a trellis set up for climbing beans. "Make a deal where they get half of the produce, or something like that."

Maggie stretched her arms over her head and paused before glancing at her watch. "We've been out here for hours."

"We must have napped longer than we thought."

"Come on." Maggie led the way out of the garden. "I want to see the barn before supper."

As they approached the large red structure, Maggie pulled out her key ring. Only the farmhouse key had a tag on it, so she tried four others before finding the right one. The lock came off quietly, but the barn doors screeched as they pulled them open.

"I thought Francois took care of things around here?" Ellie said. "That rusty hinge needs oiling."

"I'll add it to my list."

The cool air that greeted them caressed their warm cheeks as they squinted in the dim light. They entered a large area with a concrete floor. Along one side were three horse stalls, each empty and swept clean. A shiny red Chevy Corvette sat in the far corner, and next to it was a sit-down lawn mower in need of a thorough cleaning. The outside world seemed muted in the silence.

"So, this is the car my grandmother left him." Maggie ran her hand along the sides of the Corvette and peered into the driver's seat. "Very nice."

"Kinda flashy, if you ask me," Ellie said.

"You don't want Francois to get anything, do you?"

"I don't like him."

"Neither do I, but the sooner he gets what's his, the sooner he's out of my hair."

"You realize your grandmother drove this, right?" Ellie asked.

"There appears to be many sides to her. But *this* is surprising." Maggie patted the trunk of the car and continued on.

The rest of the barn contained normal farming and gardening equipment. The gardening area had well maintained tools hanging on the wall for easy access. A bench beside it held a few pots of soil and a packet of seeds.

"This must have been your grandmother's domain," Ellie said. She picked up the open packet and showed it to Maggie. "Lavender, your favorite. Looks like she just planted these."

Maggie noticed the finger indentations in the soil, as if someone had recently settled the seeds into place. She touched the spot and grabbed her water bottle. When she'd watered both pots to her satisfaction, she gathered them up and headed out.

"I'm sweaty and I'm hungry."

They left the barn just as they found it, quiet and locked.

***

After they'd each had their turn in the shower, Ellie put the meat pie in the oven for dinner. "This won't take long to heat up, and it looks delicious." After searching the cupboard, she gathered plates and utensils, and set the small table, keeping an eye on her friend.

Maggie turned slowly in a full circle, as if she wanted to imprint every piece of furniture and knick-knack on her brain for future reference. "I thought this place would be ... older."

Ellie tried to see it from Maggie's perspective. "It's tidy and quite comfortable. I think your grandmother had great taste."

Maggie took a seat at the table and leaned forward. "I guess I'm just overwhelmed by it all."

Ellie found some glasses and brought soft drinks from their cooler and sat with her. "I wonder who put all this food here. She must have had someone else she trusted to help her as well."

Maggie shook her head. "I think Francois would have told us. He seems sure that he's the only person who ever helped her."

Ellie snorted in annoyance at the mention of Maggie's cousin. "Francois thinks too highly of himself. But the assortment of food here is the work of someone who knows what they're doing."

"Maybe my grandmother left a list of things I like, because the stuff in there," Maggie waved at the refrigerator, "are things I will eat."

"And we all know what a picky eater you are!" Ellie said. The timer buzzed, and she brought the pie to the table. "Now, here is another all-time favorite, the meat pie, crispy golden crust, bubbling inside, perfection."

They ate in silence, letting the minutes pass, each tired from the property walk. Maggie turned in her seat to get a better look at one particular aspect of the farmhouse. Her eyes latched onto an old roll-top desk in a corner of the living room. Ellie followed her gaze and raised an eyebrow. "That looks ancient."

Wiping her mouth after her last bite, Maggie went over to it and pulled out drawer after drawer. Most were empty, but in the biggest one at the bottom was a sketchbook. She brought it back to the table, but Ellie motioned her to the couch by the fireplace. "Let's get comfortable first."

The two women sank down, side by side, and Maggie opened the cover of the sketchbook. The drawings were simple but elegant, with views of the farm in different seasons, the creek, the barn, birds, and other wildlife. And then a gorgeous, detailed drawing of the cabin in the woods.

Maggie gasped when she saw it, and Ellie let out a small "Wow".

The last three pages had sketches of people, the first being Maggie's mother, Florence, smiling and happy as a young girl. The second was of Maggie. "I don't remember a picture like this," she whispered.

"Then it's from memory."

"But she never saw me."

"Maybe it's time to rethink that. It's obvious she's seen you, and not just from the photos your mom sent her."

"But..."

"She was really talented." Ellie pointed at the signature on each page. A single letter— O.

Then Maggie flipped to the last page. A smiling man with a twinkle in his eyes, unruly hair, and a bushy beard.

"Now, *he's* hot!" Ellie said. "Who is he?"

Maggie leaned closer. "I've never seen him before, but—that beard. Could he be the guy in the drawings from the treehouse?" Maggie tried to stifle a yawn, but failed.

"Wait a second." Ellie stared into the man's eyes. "He reminds me of someone, but I can't put my finger on it." She took the treehouse drawings out of the backpack and spread them out on the coffee table.

They both studied them closely, then Maggie yawned again and covered her mouth with her hand. "The drawings are too vague."

Ellie checked the clock. "It may be early, but we're both exhausted. Let's get our stuff inside, find a bed, and hit the hay. We'll explore more tomorrow after a good night's sleep."

"You always say that." Maggie placed the sketchbook down on the table.

"And am I ever wrong?" Ellie called over her shoulder as she put her shoes back on and headed for the car.

"No," Maggie muttered.

***

An hour later, they were both in their pajamas, in a quaint bedroom with two single beds. There were three more bedrooms on the second floor. The largest was obviously Octavie's as it still contained her personal effects, but the others were empty except for a stripped bed and a bureau. They'd found this room set up as if they were expecting guests, everything cozy and fresh.

Ellie opened the window a crack to let in the cooler night air, then pulled Maggie onto the bed beside her. "Now, whatever we do here is on your terms. Remember that." She squeezed Maggie's hand. "You don't have to decide right now, or even in the next few weeks."

"Yes, Mom." Maggie leaned into her and sighed. "I want to take some time to see everything I've inherited. I thought we'd check out the whole house in the morning." She turned to Ellie and frowned. "And I need to get into the cabin by the creek. It's just so..."

"Exactly!" Ellie laughed. "It's just *so*." She hugged her friend and stepped over to her own bed. "Oh, and we should check out the bakery in town."

"Oh, dear," Maggie groaned. "What am I going to tell the couple who run it?"

"We'll figure it out when we get there." Ellie plumped her pillow and pulled the warm quilt over her shoulders. "This is so nice. I never had a sleepover as a kid. With friends, I mean. With my cousin, Sophie, sure, but I lived with them, so it wasn't the same."

"Me neither," Maggie said as she settled into her bed and turned on her side to face her friend. "Thanks, Ellie."

“For what?”

“For coming with me and being a calming voice in all this madness.”

“You’re welcome,” Ellie smiled at her and reached over to turn off the table lamp. “After what you did for me when Adam and Winnie died, this is peanuts. We’re in this together, kiddo.” Her awful Humphrey Bogart impression made Maggie laugh, and soon all they could hear were the crickets and the gentle wind in the trees.

Chapter Eleven

The kitchen was sparkling clean after breakfast and Maggie decided it was time to explore the top floor more thoroughly.

They paused in one of the smaller bedrooms, empty except for a single bed pressed against one wall. The large, clean window provided a wonderful view of the forest and creek at the back of the property.

Something on the far wall caught Ellie's attention. She walked over and crouched before it, running her fingers along some scratches. "Check this out." From her position, she noticed similar markings all along the wall.

Maggie joined her and squinted where Ellie pointed. "They're initials!"

Ellie nodded. "There are about ten of them in total. And look, this one has a date on it. August, 1945."

"That was during the war. Who stayed here during the war?"

Ellie didn't respond, lost in thought. "Let's check the other room."

She took off before Maggie could answer, and Maggie found her in the same crouched position in the second bedroom. Ellie's fingers traced another set of initials. "This is really weird," she muttered to herself.

Maggie pulled her up and out of the room. "Yes, you can work your detective stuff later. I want to explore my grandmother's room. That's where people keep the sentimental stuff." She nodded at Ellie. "Right?"

"And what do you keep in your bedroom?" Ellie followed Maggie into the largest bedroom.

"My diaries."

"And here I thought I was the only one who kept a journal!"

"Oh, my, but you're fancy, a journal. Mine is just a diary." Maggie stood in the middle of the room, taking it all in. The queen-size bed filled the center of the far wall, leaving plenty of room between the door and the foot of the bed. A large bay window with colorful seat cushions occupied one wall, and against the other stood a wooden bureau. A lace runner covered the top, while a bottle of perfume, a jewellery box, and a brush and comb sat at even intervals.

"She was immaculate," Ellie said.

"I did *not* inherit that trait."

Ellie ran her hand over the wallpaper, a small red carnation pattern that rose from floor to ceiling and behind the bay window. The other walls were painted pale blue, and the morning sun danced into the room, leaving a wonderful glow from the colors. "This is beautiful."

A slow smile stole across Maggie's face as the atmosphere of the room enveloped her. She opened a door, and a flick of a wall switch illuminated the interior. "Jeesh!"

Ellie peered inside. "Indeed." They both marveled at the walk-in closet, one side for hanging clothes, another with shelves for sweaters, shoes, purses, and hats. At the end hung a full-length mirror, now reflecting their wide-eyed astonishment at what they'd found.

"She certainly loved clothes," Maggie said.

Ellie stepped inside and took a closer look. "There's actually not that many." She picked out a few pieces and read the labels. "They're all excellent quality, timeless and durable."

Maggie reached up to the top shelf that ran around the three walls and grabbed a box. She caught it and stumbled out of the closet, surprised by its weight, and placed it on the bed.

"You want all the boxes out?" Ellie pointed at the shelves above. She'd need a chair to reach anything that high.

Not getting an answer, she poked her head out and saw Maggie holding a picture, her other hand clenched to her mouth, a glittering key on a chain dangling from her fingers.

"What is it?" Ellie ran out, worried.

"I found the key to the cabin." Maggie showed her the label with a fine printed word on it – "Cabin". She then held up the picture and Ellie saw a handsome man, the spitting image of Maggie. "Oh, my!" She turned it over so Ellie could read. *Graham, mon Coeur.*

"He looks like you." Ellie put an arm around Maggie's shoulders. "It's black and white, but his hair is light, maybe red?"

"My heart." Maggie couldn't take her eyes off him. "Do you think this was my grandmother's husband, mom's father, my grandfather?"

"You can't deny the resemblance. Have you ever heard of him?"

"Never."

"This is the man in the sketchbook, and all the sketches from the treehouse."

Maggie dug through the other pictures in the box, uncovering more of Graham alone, one of Graham and her grandmother standing on the cabin porch, huge smiles on their faces, and another of Graham in uniform. "I bet that cabin was their special place."

"Probably." Ellie took the picture from her and studied it. "If they weren't married, it would have been frowned upon for him to stay here, her being a single woman."

"What was he doing here in the first place? Where did he come from?"

"We'd have to do some serious investigating to get those answers."

Maggie had a twinkle in her eye as she opened her mouth.

Ellie held up her hand to stop whatever she was going to say. "One thing at a time." She stood up and glanced around. "What else do you want to go through before we head out to the cabin?

***

They spent the next two hours exploring the house and found that Octavie had kept a minimalist but comfortable home.

"It's like she knew she was dying and made sure her affairs were in order," Maggie said as she flipped through the folders in a small filing cabinet by the roll-top desk. "Everything's here, labeled and ready to go."

"I wish I had her talent!" Ellie laughed, waiting for the comments about her being a lover of piles of things instead of putting things away. When no remarks came, she turned to see Maggie staring out the window. "Right," Ellie said, clapping her hands to get her friend's attention. "It's time to visit the cabin. We need that key. Where did you put it?"

Maggie pulled it out of her pocket and held it up as if it was precious treasure. "Let's go." She headed out the front door, leaving Ellie to run after her.

The sun beat down on them as they walked through the field, the flowers fragrant in the heat of the day. They made it to the cabin quicker than the day before, and within minutes, they were standing on the porch.

Maggie put the key in the lock and turned it, worried it would not open, but when it clicked and released, she let out a whoop of excitement. She pushed it open and stepped over the threshold.

"Would you look at this!" Ellie said as she followed her inside.

The cabin was one room, two windows on opposite walls, and a small door at the back. To the left was a double bed, covered with a pale green quilt. A plain kitchen counter with a sink took up the other side, a couple of shelves above held two large plates, two cups, two of everything. And in the drying rack below were two glasses and two smaller plates. Above the sink, the curtains at the window had a bright carnation pattern, the twin of the one in the farmhouse.

Maggie skimmed her fingers over the back of one of the two kitchen chairs facing each other. A man's dark green tartan shirt rested on the back of one, and on the table was an open newspaper, an ashtray with a squashed-out cigarette, and a pen. A vase sat in the middle; any flowers it had held were long gone.

Everything was covered in a fine layer of dust.

The room felt as if its occupants had just stepped out, expecting to return soon.

Maggie leaned over and read the date on the newspaper, "June 15, 1945."

"The war was raging then," Ellie whispered.

"So, this is where they met? Their love nest?" Maggie walked over to the bed and picked up another scrapbook from an end table. She blew away the dust and opened it, surprised to find photos inside instead of drawings. She motioned for Ellie to come over and they turned each page, smiling back at more pictures of the young couple forever captured in the images.

"They were so young." Ellie ran a fingertip over a photo of Octavie and Graham sitting on the front porch of the cabin. "Those smiles are priceless."

Maggie closed the scrapbook and replaced it on the table before wandering around, touching each item, picking up books, and tucking in a wayward apron into the rack by the sink. "I'm going to assume Graham is my grandfather, Mom's dad."

Ellie watched her friend move slowly around the room. "I think that's a good assumption, but until we have proof..."

"I know!" Maggie turned to her with a smile. "Never assume. It makes an ass of you and me."

In the distance, they heard the blare of a car horn, as if held by a furious fist. It came from the farmhouse and both women looked at each other in disbelief.

"Did you lock up after we left?" Ellie asked.

"Yes, thank goodness," Maggie muttered as she locked the cabin door tight behind them before they headed back to what they feared would be another run in with Francois.

***

He was waiting for them, leaning against the hood of his car, a cigarette clenched between his teeth. His girlfriend remained in the passenger seat, refusing to turn and acknowledge them as Maggie and Ellie approached.

"Where have you been?" he demanded, as if he had a right to know her every move. "Where you at the cabin? Did you find the key and get in?"

"What can I do for you?" Maggie asked with a sigh, refusing to explain her whereabouts to Francois. She straightened her spine, preparing for another confrontation.

Francois threw his cigarette and stomped on it, grinding it into the ground. "I demand part of my inheritance now." His chin rose, as if daring her to refuse.

"How many times do I have to tell you?" Maggie pronounced each word slowly, "Speak to Notary Bouchard. I have nothing to do with the distribution. He said it would take a while."

"But I need something now."

"Why?" Ellie watched him shuffle his feet, sweat beading his forehead.

"None of your business," he snapped. He struggled to intimidate her again, taking a step towards her. But Ellie stood her ground, raising an eyebrow at his childish behavior.

"Then you can leave." Maggie walked up the porch steps before turning to him. "And don't come back here. I'll consider it trespassing."

"But... but," he stammered, thrown off guard by her dismissal. "Look." His tone turned sweet, as if he realized his mistake. "All I want to know is what we're going to do with the property? Keep it, sell it?"

We?? Maggie stared at him, stunned by his suggestion that he had any kind of say in the matter.

He pulled a card out of his pocket and tried to hand it to her. "This is my number. I understand this is overwhelming for you, but call me and we'll talk about what to do with the farm."

Ellie snatched it from him and stepped into his space. She'd always despised bullies, but the one thing she'd learned from being smaller than everyone else was that bullies were actually cowards. And Francois proved her right by stumbling away and grabbing for the car door.

"She doesn't need to discuss anything with you!" Ellie said, waving his card at him in amazement. "This *isn't* your property." She couldn't believe the gall of the guy.

Maggie stepped off the porch and took her arm, pulling her aside; eyes focused on her cousin, never wavering.

Francois slid into the car and leaned back out the window. "I'm ready to talk anytime you are." Without waiting for an answer, he waved wildly and sped off, leaving a cloud of dust in his wake.

"His creepiness is getting worse," Ellie muttered, a shiver running through her.

"Not our monkey, not our circus," Maggie said lightly, but her brow furrowed with concern.

Chapter Twelve

Maggie locked the farmhouse door behind her before joining Ellie in the driveway. Lunch had been quick, the dishes done, and they were off to visit Octavie's resting place in the town cemetery. Maggie had spent a few minutes in the wildflower garden, putting together a small bouquet of flowers for the grave.

"Walk or drive?" Ellie asked, dangling the car keys out in front of her. The afternoon sun shone off them, warming them in her fingers.

Maggie hesitated, remembering the manageable distance from the church to her grandmother's property. "A hundred percent walk." She smiled at Ellie and off they went.

Strangely, the driveway didn't feel as long as Ellie remembered it being yesterday, but it still took them almost five minutes to get to the end. For that amount of time at least, they enjoyed the shade of the tree tunnel. Seeing no traffic, they stepped out onto the dirt road and headed towards the church.

"I could get used to this," Ellie said, gazing at the fields that lined both sides of the road. They could see other farms at the end of long, open driveways. Corn stalks covered acres of land, with patches of apple trees closer to the homes.

"It *is* amazing," Maggie agreed, taking a deep breath of clean air and enjoying the heat of the sun on her bare arms.

Noting the church spire in the distance, they covered the distance in half an hour. Since the town itself lay on the other side of the church and cemetery, they would not have to walk down the main street, yet.

They strolled through an open gate into the cemetery behind the modest church and hesitated. The grounds were much larger than they had expected. A well-worn path led from the back side through a small grove of trees and into another portion where more tombstones gleamed in the sun.

"Where do we start?" Maggie asked.

Ellie scanned the area, then pointed to the other side. "See that one over there, near the bushes? That looks recent. Let's try that first."

"I never would have thought of that," Maggie murmured, following behind.

They stepped around tombstones, treading only at the foot end of a grave. Not that the occupants cared, but Ellie had always felt strongly about doing so.

When they reached the new grave, they spotted a small house behind the bushes, as if nestled between the two parts of the cemetery and the church itself. Ellie shielded her eyes and peered closer. An older woman was watching them from the porch. She raised her hand and waved, and Ellie and Maggie waved back.

"This is it," Maggie whispered, looking at the headstone that bore her grandmother's name and dates. "Wow, she was old!"

"Octavie Duprat. Born in 1917, almost smack dab in the middle of the first war."

"Would that mean her father didn't serve?" Maggie said.

"Not necessarily. He could have been on leave when she was conceived, or too old, or injured."

"Another mystery?" Maggie joked.

"With your family mysteries, you'll soon be my only client!"

"What is written at the bottom of the stone?"

"It's in French." Ellie read the carving easily, for only a few weeds had had time to take root. A bunch of colorful wildflowers sat in a simple plastic vase at the base of the stone, and Maggie placed her own bouquet next to it.

"I should be able to read it myself. Give me a second."

"How come you never learned to speak French?" Ellie asked.

“Mom never spoke it at home, Dad never picked it up, and I never actually had to use it. Which is no excuse, I know.” Maggie admitted. “Okay. It says “*lache ma poitrine*”. Which means...”

Ellie let out a hoot, bracing her hands on her knees from the strength of her laughing. “It means get off my chest.” Tears streamed down her face as Maggie shook her head in disbelief.

“I guess she had a sense of humor,” Maggie smiled, resting her hand on top of the tombstone.

“Oh, gosh, that’s perfect!” Ellie wiped her eyes and looked over at the old woman on the nearby porch, worried that her laughter would seem rude. But the woman gave her a thumbs up before disappearing into her house.

“Okay.” Maggie caught Ellie’s gaze on the path to the other part of the cemetery. “Should I you here to explore and pick you up on the way back from town?”

“You want to go now?”

“Why not?” Maggie shrugged. “Might as well get this over with.’

“I can’t wait to see what the Tavie Bakery looks like.”

They headed back to where the gate met the main street, and continued along, noting how the homes and businesses became more numerous.

“I’m a bit nervous, to be honest,” Maggie said, swatting a mosquito away from her head. “What if they think I’m going to take over, or change everything?”

Ellie linked her arm with her friend’s again and squeezed it for support. “We’ll go and check things out. No one needs to know who you are.”

“Of course,” Maggie said, relieved. “No one knows who I am!”

***

As they strolled along the quaint main street of St. Anne de Lafont, they quickly realized how wrong they were. They passed a butcher shop, a grocery store, a tailor, a barber shop, and the town hall and library, which were housed together in an old house. And at the end of the road, they saw the sign for Boulangerie Tavie Bakery.

But as they passed people on the street, they wondered why they were attracting stares. Maggie and Ellie returned the smiles and bonjours that came their way from strangers, and when they arrived at her grandmother's bakery with the iconic sign, they realized why everyone seemed so interested in them. The window held pictures through the years of the building and of Octavie herself. When Octavie Duprat was younger, she looked like Maggie, but with dark hair.

Maggie peered past the pictures and into the bakery. A young couple stood behind the counter, frozen as they stared back at her. "Oh, hell's bells," she muttered. "They know who I am."

Ellie pushed open the door and stepped inside. Maggie followed, dragging her feet in dread. But the smells that greeted her were like walking into her own Cozy Corner Café and instantly comforting.

Maggie lifted her head and sniffed deeply, causing the two older customers at the counter to widen their eyes in surprise. "It's the spices," she said under her breath, "definitely the spices."

"Mon dieu," said one lady as she took her purchase from the counter. "C'est Octavie!"

Ellie smiled at the confusion. "Non, c'est la petite fille de Octavie."

Another woman approached Maggie. "You look just like your grandmother. Oh, excuse me," she apologized in broken English. "I am... shocked." She reached out to touch Maggie's red hair. "You have her face. Pas le – not the hair!" She laughed, trying to communicate.

"Come, Marie." The other woman pulled her friend along, managing to get her own fair share of looks at Maggie. "They must have business to attend to."

They left the bakery, closing the door gently behind them. The silence lingered until the young woman behind the counter straightened her shoulders, pushed back her dark hair, and came around, hand outstretched. "Welcome." She took Maggie's hand and shook it. "We are so pleased to meet you. I'm Veronique and this is Samuel." Her accent colored her words with a delightful lilt.

Her partner came around the counter, and shook Maggie's hand as well, looking at her as if expecting the worst.

"It smells heavenly in here!" Maggie grinned, checking out the small customer area. The shop part of the business was the size of a living room. Counters lined the two opposite walls; one was filled with baskets of assorted breads, cookies, and muffins. The other wall showcased the Tavie Bakery's signature apple pie, while display cases next to the counter held the specialties, including eclairs, macaroons, and financiers. Each was grouped on colorful doilies on delicate Wedgewood platters. The effect was stunning.

A large window behind the main counter allowed everyone to see where the baking magic happened in the room beyond. A middle-aged woman was busily kneading dough, a strand of hair escaping from her cap as she stole glances at them. Maggie waved and smiled. The woman froze, then hesitantly raised a hand before returning to her work.

"Did you know I'd be coming?" Maggie turned to the couple and tried for another friendly smile, but her nerves turned it into a wobble.

"Yes," Veronique hesitated, as if dreading whatever their fate would be. "Octavie told us you would, we just didn't know when."

"Do you know the whole story about Maggie and her grandmother?" Ellie wondered how much more awkward this could get.

"Only that she was very proud of you and said you were a baker not to be trifled with," Samuel replied with a smile, as if remembering a conversation that had brought him pleasure. "Oh, and she left you something. Come and see the baking room."

They followed him into the rear. The cleanliness and organization of the whole layout impressed Maggie. The ovens lined one wall, and the prep island filled the middle of the floor, allowing everyone to work around it. One wall held shelves of ingredients, and another lower open cabinet held boxes and bags with her grandmother's smiling face looking back at her.

"This is quite something." Ellie leaned against the wall, trying to stay out of the way.

"It really is," Maggie agreed. "You've both done a great job here."

"Octavie trusted us," Veronique said, jamming her hands into her pockets, perhaps to keep herself from wringing her fingers.

Maggie impulsively leaned over and gave her a quick hug. "I know," Maggie said. "She left me a letter telling me what you've accomplished here and how lucky she was to have found you both."

Samuel handed her an envelope. "And this is for you. She asked that we put it directly in your hands when you came."

Maggie raised an eyebrow in question.

"We have no idea what it is." Veronique shrugged, though her curiosity showed in the way her eyes kept returning to the envelope in Maggie's hands.

"So," Samuel rubbed his hands together. "I suppose you want to go over the books and the orders and..."

Maggie shoved the envelope into her pocket. "No! Oh, gosh no. That's okay, there'll be time for that later."

"But you must want to know how the business is doing before you sell it," Veronique lowered her head, waiting for the answer.

"Of course, I want to know how the business is doing." Maggie took her time, absorbing every aspect of the large workroom and the items in it. "But I haven't thought about selling it." She turned back to the couple. "I'll come back and we'll talk more, but I would never sell it from under you."

The tension in Veronique's shoulders released, as if a plug had been pulled and the stress had been released from her body. A radiant smile lit up her face, and she sagged against the table. "Oh, thank goodness."

Maggie gave her shoulder a reassuring squeeze. "For now, carry on as you have. Nothing has changed."

"Excuse me." Samuel walked past them into the shop. They turned to find the room had filled with customers, each trying not to show their interest in the red-haired woman in the back. But Maggie determinedly met the eyes of each curious customer and smiled at them.

"There are a lot of people who would love to meet Octavie's granddaughter," Veronique said. "Would you mind?" She walked into the store and looked back at Maggie. She hadn't moved. "They were her friends, and they miss her."

Ellie took Maggie's elbow and led her forward. She leaned into her friend and whispered, "What a great way to learn about her!"

***

Four elderly residents were waiting for Maggie to enter the room. One gentleman stood by the front door, as if about to make a quick getaway, but his eyes never left Maggie's face. She glanced at him and smiled, but was startled when he frowned back at her.

"Je dois te dire, ma chere," the tallest of the three women said as she reached out and took Maggie's hand.

"Excuse us, everyone," Veronique said. "Maggie's French is not up to our quick comments."

"Oh, I'm sorry," the tall woman said, still gripping Maggie's fingers as if afraid the young woman would run away if she let go. "I was going to say you look so much like your grandmother."

"Except for the hair," another woman piped up, peering from around her friend's shoulder.

"I think we know where that came from," the frowning man in the corner said in a deep, disapproving voice.

"Luc." The first woman shook her head at him.

He grunted, pushed through the front door, and left.

"Don't mind him." The tiny woman rescued Maggie's hand from her friend's grip and smiled at her. "It's so lovely to meet you. I'm Marie. We grew up with your grandmother. We have so much to tell you!"

"Well, I..." Maggie felt her stomach sink, overwhelm sliding down her body, even though they all seemed pleased to meet her.

"Dear." The third woman pushed her long grey hair away from her face. "Your grandmother was a wonderful woman. She helped many people in this town."

"Those who *let* her help them," Marie said with a shake of her head, as if she couldn't believe that anyone would not let Octavie help them.

The taller woman nodded in agreement. "And she had a great sense of humor."

Silence surrounded them. "Well," Maggie said. "I'll be back in a few weeks to sort things out, and I'd love to sit and talk with you all. I'm sure you have a lot of stories to share about my grandmother."

"Oh, my," said the tiny woman, "that would be lovely!"

"I'll get everyone's name and number from Veronique and be in touch," Maggie said, nodding as if to convince herself that it was a good plan. "We'll have a tea at the farm."

"Oh," the tall woman whispered, "could we see the cabin?"

Ellie laughed from her place behind the counter. "And what do you know about the cabin?"

The women all shuffled together, refusing to look at Maggie, but then Marie turned to her, a twinkle in her eye. "That's where the greatest romance blossomed."

Veronique chose that moment to sweep in and open the front door for the women. "That's all for now, then," she said, her brisk tone stopping any further conversation. "I'll give Maggie your numbers and you can all gossip when she gets back."

"But it's not gossip if it's true," the tall woman admonished as she walked out, taking a moment to wave to Maggie as she left.

"Nice to meet you all," Maggie called out to their departing backs, waving as they all turned to catch one last look.

Veronique closed the door behind them. "Sorry about that."

"Not at all," Maggie said with a laugh, though she leaned against the counter for some strength. "I'm pretty sure my grandmother had a man in her life named Graham."

"And he had red hair," Ellie added.

"But beyond that, I don't know anything else for sure," Maggie admitted.

Veronique and Samuel exchanged glances, but their lips remained sealed.

Maggie checked her watch and jumped with a start. "Okay, we have got to get back to finish our exploration before we leave tomorrow." She touched her pocket to make sure the envelope was safe, then held out her hand to the young couple. "Please, don't worry. All I ask is that you continue as you are."

When Samuel took her hand, he held it longer than necessary. "And all we ask is that if you decide to sell, you give us the first chance."

"That sounds more than fair," Maggie nodded. "I'll be back soon, and we'll talk."

"And if you have any questions, call," Veronique said as she opened the door once more to let them out.

Maggie stepped outside into the fresh air, air that did not smell as comforting as the aromas in the bakery. It felt like leaving a safe cocoon.

Ellie slipped her arm through Maggie's again, and turned her toward the church and the road back to the farm.

Chapter Thirteen

The clouds rolled in quickly as they walked past the church and along the road, and by the time they reached the head of the driveway, the rain had begun. They ran laughing down its long, windy gravel surface, arriving on the porch soaking wet.

"That was such fun!" Ellie said, wringing out her hair.

"It's like being a kid again." Maggie opened the front door, and they both piled in, water dripping onto the front carpet. "Let me get some towels." She slipped out of her shoes and walked barefoot to the downstairs powder room, returning with two towels. She tossed one to Ellie and wrapped the other around her head before they went upstairs to change.

Maggie remembered to take the envelope out of her back pocket before she took off her shorts.

"Is it wet?" Ellie asked.

Maggie turned it over and checked. "Not a drop on it."

"Are you going to open it or what?"

Maggie looked up and nodded. "In a minute. It's like a Schrödinger's Cat situation. I'm full of hope for what might be inside, but I might be disappointed if I open it."

Ellie finished changing and draped her clothes over a chair. She took the envelope, though Maggie's hand remained outstretched as if she would grab it back. "Get changed and meet me downstairs. Adventure is afoot." Ellie held the envelope in the air as she ran out, sure that Maggie would be minutes behind.

She sat on the comfortable couch in the living room, tapping her fingers against her knee as Maggie ran into the room. The envelope lay on the table like a golden gift, and Maggie seized it before sitting down. She gave Ellie a half grin, unsure of what to do.

"I swear, Margaret Catherine Williams, if you don't open it right now, I'll do it for you!"

Maggie stuck her finger in the flap and carefully slit it open. She pulled out a letter and a handful of recipe cards.

Ellie sat forward and tried to read the writing on the top card. "Sweet potato cupcakes with brown sugar frosting? That sounds delicious."

Maggie sat back, opened the letter, and read aloud.

"*My dearest Maggie, If you are reading this, I am sorry that we never knowingly met in person. And that was my fault. Never blame your mother. I drove her away from home. I never knew your father, but I can tell he was a wonderful husband and father. You are the proof of that.*"

Maggie looked up in disbelief. "What could she have done to make her own daughter disown her?" She resumed reading.

"*As stated in my will, I've left you my estate, with the exception of a few gifts for your cousin, Francois. I hope he will behave, but believe me when I tell you that his bark is worse than his bite. My pride is the farm. You thought it was the Tavie Bakery? The business kept me busy, but my love was the farm. You don't see much there, but it has a history. And the cabin is my heart.*"

"Graham?" Ellie asked. "Does she name him or say who he is?"

Maggie held up a hand and scanned the letter. "No."

"*I left you something else, some recipes that have never been part of the Tavie Bakery business. They are my own special concoctions, and I want you to have them. From one baker to another. Do with them what you will.*"

Maggie stopped reading and scrutinized the cards in her hand. She flipped through them and counted twelve unique recipes. "Oh, my gosh!" She glanced through them, stopping at one, going back to another. "These are amazing, Ellie." She handed them to her friend and returned to the letter.

"I have so much to tell you, and I will. I know how overwhelming this must be for you. For now, I hope this brings you some joy. Your loving Grandmere."

"What does she mean she'll share more with me later?" Maggie checked out the back of the pages, hoping for more information, but they were blank.

"Maybe she died before she could finish what she wanted to tell you," Ellie said. "Or...maybe she wanted to meet you in person."

"That's another thing," Maggie went back to the letter. "Here she says she's sorry we never *knowingly* met in person. What the heck does that mean?"

"We may never know."

Maggie frowned and Ellie wished there was something she could do for her friend. "Look at this." Ellie waved a recipe card. "It's dark chocolate mousse cake. Oh, please, please, make this for me!"

Maggie knew what Ellie was up to, but she took the card from her and read the directions. "There's one ingredient in this that *will* make it amazing."

"I know nothing about baking, oh great one." Ellie gave her a deep bow. "I bet you can make this. For me. Please."

Maggie headed for the kitchen, studying the recipe as she went. "Let me see if my grandmother has all the ingredients here."

"There could be a Percyville Bake Fair Contest winning recipe in there!" Ellie watched Maggie pause as a slow grin spread across her face before she disappeared into the kitchen.

For the next hour, Ellie relaxed on the couch, pen and notebook in hand, as she made numerous bullet points about what she wanted to research for Maggie. She paused occasionally to watch the rain patter against the window and listen to her best friend hum as she pulled out pots and pans to bake a recipe her grandmother had created for her.

***

Ellie's moans of pleasure followed her first bite of Octavie's dark chocolate mousse cake. Supper was finished and dessert had been placed on the table in front of Ellie with great ceremony. It was exceptional, and she had a second piece, knowing she'd pay for it later with a rough night's sleep. Sweets did that to her, but they were her greatest weakness, and she fought them every day, sometimes winning, but more often losing.

They cleaned up and retired to the living room after packing everything they could for the morning trip back home.

The knock on the front door startled them both, but Maggie made no move forward. "Francois again?" She looked at Ellie, but Ellie just shrugged.

Chapter Fourteen

Maggie finally made it to the door, Ellie trailing behind her. She turned on the outside light, and there on the balcony, in a dim pool of light, stood a tiny old woman holding a pie plate.

"Bonjour, hi." The woman smiled at them through the screen door; her shoulders hunched forward as if the pie weighed her down.

"Oh, please, come in." Maggie opened the door and took the plate from the woman's outstretched hands. "Thank you."

The woman stepped inside, glancing around as if searching for someone. She turned to Maggie and took her free hand. "I am sorry for your loss," she said, her English impeccable though tinged with a French accent. "I'm Louise Ethier." As Maggie shook the woman's hand and led her into the living room, Ellie swooped in and took the pie from her friend.

"Thank you," Maggie said, motioning for the woman to take the most comfortable chair in the room.

"Oh, no," Louise said, settling herself instead in the farthest corner of the big couch. "*This* is my seat." Her feet dangled above the floor.

Maggie and Ellie stood rooted to the spot, unsure how to proceed.

"Sit, sit." Louise patted the couch beside her. Maggie sat there while Ellie took the chair across from them. "I wanted to come and tell you about your grandmother. You must have so many questions. She and I have been friends since we were little girls. We both went to university in Montreal and took secretarial courses. She returned here when her aunt died, and she inherited this farm, but

I stayed in Montreal for a while. I finally came back when my mother died, near the end of the war, and helped Octavie where I could. I was also the one who found her body at the cabin, in her hammock." She clasped her hands together and waited. She seemed unaware that her story had jumped from the distant past to the present, leaving Maggie and Ellie both totally confused and curious about the important parts left out of the whirlwind summary of Octavie's life.

"Oh, my." Maggie took in a shocked breath. "I'm so sorry you had to go through that."

"I'm glad it was me," she looked at the walking stick in the corner. "I see you found her stability helper. Or at least that's what she called it. Couldn't bear to call it a cane!"

Ellie squinted at her as a thought struck. "Are you the lady who lives in the house by the cemetery?"

"Yes," Louise smiled. "I saw you at her grave, but I didn't want to disturb you."

"Did you know that I've never met my grandmother?" Maggie wondered if this woman knew the whole story.

"Octavie was always a very private woman," Louise smoothed out an invisible crease from her dress, searching for words that might help. "I never pried, but I found out the basics."

"And who was Graham?" Ellie asked.

Louise turned to her and paused before placing a hand on her chest. "He was her heart." The words hung between them, as if each woman had deciphered the meaning in her own way.

"Did they get married?" Maggie asked, fairly certain of the answer.

"Let me tell you about that time." Louise leaned back against the plump cushions.

"Oh, dear!" Maggie shot out of her seat. "I'm such a terrible host. Can I get you something, tea, coffee?"

"Sit, sit," Louise reached out and pulled Maggie down beside her. She kept their fingers intertwined. "I'm fine, thank you." She stared at Maggie until the younger woman fidgeted in her seat. "Forgive me, but you look like Octavie at your age. But not the..." she reached out and touched Maggie's red curls. "This is more like..."

"Graham's hair?" Ellie asked. She sat forward in her chair, arms on her knees, sure that a great romantic story was about to unfold. And she was a sucker for romance.

"So," Louise began, sitting back and releasing Maggie's hand. "During World War II this farm was used as a rest home for soldiers."

Maggie looked around the room, seeing it from a different angle, imagining soldiers filling the space.

"For the injured Canadian fighters from this area," Louise continued. "They came here and the doctors examined them before sending them on their way."

"Maybe those were the initials we found in the bedrooms!" Ellie nodded to herself, as if a piece of the puzzle had just fallen into place.

"Was Graham injured?" Maggie asked.

"No. A rich man hired him to bring the man's son home." Louise rubbed two fingers together in the age-old sign of having money. "Octavie told me that Graham was from the Maritimes. His people came here from Scotland before he was born. Oh, and he was a doctor."

"Someone hired Graham to leave the war and bring his son home? Is that even possible?" Ellie asked.

"I don't know the details, only that he was here," Louise said. "The rich man arrived within a day and took his son home."

"And Graham stayed?" Maggie asked.

"No, he went back," Louise said.

"Right away?" Ellie asked.

"No." Louise glanced at Maggie and smiled. "He only stayed a month before he was called back. They only had four weeks together."

"What happened to Graham?" Maggie asked.

"She received one letter and then never heard from him again." Louise frowned; the memories obviously painful. "So, the house was in good shape when you got here?" The change of subject surprised the younger women. "I bought what I thought you would like to eat, and my niece cleaned and prepared a room for you."

"Everything was perfect." Maggie leaned back on the couch. "Thank you so much."

Maggie accepted the change of topic, but Ellie did not. "And what about the cabin out by the creek?" she asked.

"Octavie locked it up the day Graham left. If she returned to it, I don't know. I stayed with her after that, just to be there for her. Neither of us ever married, and I worked at the church, keeping the records. We were like sisters, but we kept our own homes."

"What about her own family?" Ellie asked. "Her parents and siblings?"

Louise looked down at her hands and sighed. "When Octavie inherited this farm and chose to live here, her parents wanted nothing to do with her. They thought she should marry, have children, that was her lot in life. Or so they thought."

"That would have been what, the 1940s?" Ellie asked.

"She was eighteen when she inherited," Louise said, smiling at the memory. "She left home as soon as she could, to go to university, and then returned and stayed here all her life."

"But what happened to her family? Where did they live?" Maggie's hands fluttered about in her excitement.

"Her parents never spoke to her again, but her youngest sister, Helene, came to see her after her parents died. She was delightful, was Helene, and Octavie wanted her to move in with her and Florence, but old habits wouldn't allow Helene to live with a fallen woman."

"My goodness, what nonsense!" Ellie said.

"Sadly, Helene died not long after her parents. Cancer." Louise looked lost in thought for a moment, then she eased off the couch. "Have you seen the family portrait?"

Maggie and Ellie looked at each other, eyes wide open. They watched as Louise walked around the living room, staring at all the photos on the wall. Maggie stood up and followed her.

"I've never seen such a picture," Maggie said.

"Here!" Louise pointed to an ornate picture frame on the wall by the front window.

Maggie took it off the wall and held it up for Ellie to see. "It's a picture of flowers."

"Open the back," Louise instructed.

Within minutes, the back was off and the hidden image was revealed. It was Octavie and her family.

"I remember when this photo was taken. It was quite an event," Louise said, returning to her seat. "Octavie was about fourteen in that picture."

"I guess she couldn't throw it away," Maggie said quietly.

"Oh, no," Louise agreed. "She loved her family deeply, but she understood how they felt. She was strong, determined, and always open to them coming to her. They never did."

"That is so sad," Ellie said.

"Wait a minute," Maggie blurted out louder than expected. "What about my mother?"

"Little Florence?" Louise smiled at her. "Oh, she was a devil, that one. I told Octavie she spoiled her. She liked to get her own way, but Octavie did the best she could as a single parent. I accepted what happened with Florence, but a lot of people did not. There was talk, rumours, comments, but most didn't listen. Then Octavie opened Boulangerie Tavie and helped many people in the community in countless ways. Florence helped her mother quite a bit until..."

"Until?" Ellie waited for her to continue.

"Until Florence got up and left." Louise shook her head and turned back to Maggie. "Why did she leave?"

Maggie took a sharp breath as a key piece of information slipped through her fingers. Her shoulders slumped and her hope faded. "I have no idea."

***

Ellie dashed into the kitchen, sliced the pie and placed pieces on three plates before returning to the living room in record time. She didn't want to miss a minute of the conversation.

"I always think better when I eat. Thank you, dear," Louise murmured as she took a plate from Ellie.

"Oh, my goodness." Ellie closed her eyes after the first bite and let the pie melt in her mouth. "That is the best apple pie I've ever had. Sorry, Maggie, but it's true."

Maggie took a bite and her eyes popped open. She turned to Louise. "This tastes like..."

Louise grinned at her, held her plate up and nodded. "Octavie gave me this recipe. It's hers, but with my own twist."

"Let me guess," Maggie took another bite, moving the apples and crust around her mouth. "Is that ginger?"

"Indeed it is!" Louise seemed pleased with Maggie's ability to decipher the flavor. "Your grandmother loved to experiment with ingredients."

"Louise." Ellie placed her empty plate on the coffee table and sat back, not at all ashamed to have practically inhaled the piece of pie. "If you're the keeper of church records, then you must have seen Florence's birth certificate, right?"

"A flood destroyed the original records before I started working there." Louise placed her uneaten pie on the table. "The second copy is in the archives, though it's all on the computer now. We can't have another disaster destroy them again. But you can send for a copy, or check the Drouin records online."

Ellie pulled out her phone. "Nuts!"

"What?" Maggie asked.

"I've run out of data."

"Well, it wouldn't matter," Louise said. "Octavie never had internet here. At the bakery, yes, for business, but the farm is in what they call a dead space. The municipality promised us a tower in the area, with high speed. I'll believe it when I see it."

"You'll have to be patient, Ellie," Maggie said, suppressing her own disappointment. "We'll check tomorrow when we get home."

Ellie tossed her phone onto the cushion beside her and slumped back in her seat.

"Did you know that your grandmother hated driving?" Louise asked out of the blue.

"I didn't know *anything* about her," Maggie said.

"Well, she knew everything about you." Louise reached over and patted Maggie's knee. "She came to your graduation. She drove all the way to the city and secretly took pictures. She was so proud. You were beautiful."

Maggie turned to Ellie, and they both raised their eyebrows in surprise. "How did she..." Maggie said.

"You've met Notary Bouchard?" Louise grinned at her, her shoulders hunched as if sharing a secret. "He was a dear friend of your grandmother's. He wanted to be more, but Octavie wouldn't hear of it. Her heart was spoken for long ago."

"Was my mother aware of this?" Maggie asked.

"I doubt it. They hadn't spoken in years."

"And you have no idea why?"

"No, but whatever caused the rift between them haunted Octavie for the rest of her life."

"And what can you tell us about my cousin Francois?" Maggie asked.

"Distant cousin." Louise studied her. "Is he bothering you?"

"He claimed he was helping out here and thought he was getting the whole estate," Ellie said. "He gives me the willies."

Louise nodded. "I understand, but Francois is harmless. Octavie told me she left him some things in her will that would make him happy. But she didn't think he could take care of the farm or the bakery, so that's all he got."

"He's been hounding me for his share of the inheritance, but I keep referring him to Notary Bouchard," Maggie said.

"As you should." Louise appeared deep in thought. "Francois had a hard life, lots of family, but he never seemed to fit in. Octavie took pity on him and let him do some work on the farm for her. She didn't approve of his friends though, and forbid them to come here."

"Why is that?" Maggie felt a slight knot in her stomach, her instinct telling her to listen carefully to the answer.

"They're not good people, troublemakers. I don't think Francois is involved, but one wonders."

Maggie and Ellie exchanged worried glances.

"I was wondering," Ellie said, leaning towards the older woman. "Are you responsible for how clean the treehouse is?"

"Oh, I'm so glad you went there!" Louise grinned. "That would be my niece's doing. Octavie let her play there when she was young, and she made it her mission to keep it pristine for Octavie."

"I found my grandmother's drawings," Maggie said softly.

"She was very talented." Louise stood up and gathered her things. "And now, I must go. It's past my bedtime."

"Can I drive you home?" Maggie asked, glancing out the window to see the sun setting behind the trees in her forest. *Her* forest! Imagine that.

"Heavens, no!" Louise hugged her tightly before heading for the door. "I've walked home from here many times. It keeps me young." She paused and turned. "I hope to see you again though, if you come back."

"I will definitely come back," Maggie said as she held the door open for Louise, wanting to hug her again, as if that would keep a connection between her and her grandmother. "And I'll stop and visit."

Louise took her time on the stairs, then disappeared down the driveway. The air was clear after the rain and the heat had subsided. Maggie and Ellie stood on the porch, watching the stars slowly arrive in the sky.

Ellie fidgeted, then said, “We could go to the bakery and use their internet.”

Maggie put her arm around her friend’s shoulders and hugged her tightly. “Unlike you, my dear Ellie, I have patience. Tomorrow will be fine. Let’s go to sleep.”

“But it’s not dark yet,” Ellie complained, only to stifle a huge yawn as they moved back inside.

Chapter Fifteen

Maggie woke before Ellie and left the bedroom on tiptoe, holding her clothes in one hand, and easing the door closed behind her with the other. She freshened up in the bathroom, dressed, and headed out to the cabin for one last look before they headed home after breakfast.

The sun crested the trees in the distance, and the grass was damp from the night's dew. She pulled her sweater tight around her neck, and took her time walking along the path to the creek and over the small bridge to the cabin beyond. She ran her hand along the wooden railing, feeling the rough wood scratch her fingers.

Birds sang overhead as she stepped onto the porch, and a squirrel chattered at her from the balcony railing before scurrying around the side of the house. Tree branches blocked most of the rising sun and the cabin seemed shrouded in a cocoon.

She took the key from her pocket and let herself in. Suddenly, the sun broke through the leaves and illuminated the interior of the room with a startling brightness. A movie set couldn't have had better timing.

The sunlight shone off the glasses on the table and the coffeepot on the stove, even though they remained covered in dust. She wiped a spot from the quilt, revealing vibrant greens. She'd seen the same hues before, and it took a moment to recognize them, repeated in the shirt on the back of the chair.

They must be Graham's colors! Maybe the quilt had been made after he left, or while he was here, or—she stopped her imagination from running wild. She might never know the answers to her questions, but she could dream. Without a second thought, she took the shirt off the back of the chair and stepped outside to shake out the dust before rolling it up tightly and taking it with her.

Maggie found breakfast waiting when she returned to the farmhouse. They ate quickly, then Ellie took their dishes to the sink. "I'll do these while you go pack." She motioned to the front door where her own suitcase waited. "I did a tour of the house and everything's locked up tight."

Maggie gave her a big hug. "Thanks for this, Ellie. I don't think I could have faced this alone."

"You could have." Ellie squeezed Maggie's arm. "I'm just happy to be here to help. And it's such a fascinating genealogical mystery!"

Maggie rolled her eyes and ran upstairs to pack, Graham's shirt tucked under her arm. "Trust you to find adventure in dead people."

***

The dashboard clock read seven-thirty as they threw their bags in the back seat and drove down the driveway. The sun's rays created a strobe light effect through the trees until they reached the open road and turned toward town. As they passed the church, Ellie leaned out of the window to catch a glimpse of the part of the cemetery they had not visited.

"I promise, you'll see it next time," Maggie said. "We'll stay longer."

They spent the next hours chatting about what they had found, first impressions of Veronique, Samuel, and Louise. The miles passed and the conversation turned to companionable silence.

"Have you thought about what you want to do with the farmhouse?" Ellie asked out of the blue.

"Not yet. I might turn it into a B&B or use it as a vacation spot."

"You should bring Pete up here. He'd love all the old wood and architecture." Ellie let her hand hang out the window, idly catching the wind as they drove. "Speaking of Pete, how is my cousin, really?"

Maggie didn't answer right away, but Ellie caught her grinning when she looked over. "Haven't we covered all this already? Okay, I'll play. Pete's quite nice," Maggie said.

"So is my dentist, but I wouldn't kiss him." Ellie laughed. "Does he meet your high standards?"

"Look who's talking!"

"I hope for three things in a man," Ellie announced. She held out a finger. "First, he must have a sense of humor." Another finger popped out. "Second, he must be kind." The third finger popped out, and she wriggled an eyebrow at Maggie. "And last, but not least, he must be easy on *my* eyes."

"That last one is very shallow, but Quinn seems to check all your boxes to a T."

"He does," Ellie said quietly, as if to herself.

"So, what's taking so long to get from the friend part of this show?"

Ellie didn't answer.

"I'm sorry, El," Maggie said. "None of my business."

"No, no, it's okay."

Maggie grimaced. "Ever since Adam died, I've been... reluctant to bring up anything like this."

"And you have no idea how much I appreciate you letting me get here at my own pace," Ellie said.

"I'm not pushing you. We both know how well that works!"

"Actually." Ellie turned to face her friend, the seatbelt tugging at her neck. "Actually," she repeated, taking her time to find the right words. "I might be ready to move on to the next stage."

Maggie tapped the wheel with delight. "About time. What changed your mind?"

"He's never pushed me on anything." Ellie brought up her finger count again and reeled off the reasons, throwing out a finger each time. "He's funny. Check. He lives in my house and works on his projects in the barn, and it drives me crazy seeing him every day. We like the same kind of movies, and that's a bonus. We're both cuddlers. He loves Cali, and she loves him, but what dog wouldn't? He smells great, and ... he makes me happy." She said the last one with surprise, as if having just discovered that fact.

"Not his kissing skills?" Maggie joked.

"Oh, gosh, yes." Ellie leaned back and stared out the window, a slow smile turning into a wide grin. "I never thought I'd meet someone, or be willing to deal with that kind of pain again."

"You have to feel that kind of love to feel anything at all," Maggie pointed out.

They drove in silence for a while, each deep in their own thoughts. "So, what about you?" Ellie refused to drop the subject. "Is Pete someone you'd like to move forward with, or is this just a fling?"

"He's the cat's pajamas. We've both found good guys, guys we could grow old with." Maggie said. "So why do I feel guilty about being so happy?"

"What do you mean?"

"I think about my grandmother and Graham," Maggie said, pulling off the highway into the parking lot of the Cozy Corner Café. "They only had a month together, and here I am with my whole life ahead of me."

"She would be so happy for you," Ellie said as Maggie's phone rang.

Maggie answered it with a quick, "Hey, Dad." She listened for a moment, nodded, and signed off with a "Thanks, that's okay."

"No luck?" Ellie asked.

"Nope." Maggie put her phone away as Daphne stepped out of the front door and waited for her. "He couldn't find Mom's birth certificate."

"Will you come over and look at the Drouin collection with me?" Ellie asked as she got her backpack out of the car.

Maggie hesitated. "Isn't there a genealogy meeting tonight?"

"Yes." Ellie leaned against the car.

"How about we do it then and let everybody join?"

"Can you wait that long?"

"I'm more worried about you!" Maggie said.

"Patience is my middle name."

Maggie snorted in response and watched as Ellie dashed across the highway and disappeared into the hidden entrance to the woods at the back of her property. She turned to Daphne and the young woman held the door open for her.

"Today is the last day you can sign up to enter a baked good in the..." Daphne began.

"Do you have the papers?" Maggie walked past her and dropped her bags under the counter. "I have the perfect recipe for this year!" Her eyes lit up and her smile was so infectious that Daphne grinned back.

She reached behind her and handed Maggie a single sheet of paper. "If you fill it out now, I can run over to the office and make sure it's registered."

Maggie filled out the information with a flourish, believing that she might have a winning recipe to compete with. She handed the paper to Daphne and watched as she rushed to her car and drove off. Bless that girl, Maggie thought. She believes in me more than I do.

Even though people raved about her pastries, Maggie hadn't quite reached a level of self-confidence in her ability to bake. She knew she was good, but a twinge of uncertainty crept its way into her mind as she realized that people might now compare her to Tavie Bakery. Would winning a blue-ribbon be enough to make her feel like a real baker? Probably not.

But it couldn't hurt.

After tying on her apron and washing her hands, Maggie knelt at the prep counter to get the flour and sugar from the lower storage bins. As her eyes came to rest on the countertop, she saw a bright blue envelope sitting in the corner, out of reach of the crumbs, as if resting in its own circle of calm.

Rising slowly, she reached for it. A yellow sticky note fluttered on the front. "*Your Grandmother asked me to give you this. Sorry you were not here, but your éclair was divine. Jean-Pierre Bouchard.*"

She tore off the note and read the inscription on the envelope.

"*My Darling Granddaughter Marguerite.*"

Chapter Sixteen

The front door of the Café swung open and hit the wall with a thud.

"Sorry." Shirley grabbed the door and looked behind it, as if searching for holes.

Maggie stuffed the blue envelope into her apron pocket and turned to face Shirley, whose 93-year-old shoulders slumped, but whether from age or struggling with the large folder she was holding, that was the mystery.

"I've got some ideas for the front of the Café," she gasped, out of breath as she sat down at the nearest table and opened the folder before Maggie had even joined her.

"I'm sure whatever you choose will be wonderful," Maggie said.

"Maggie." Shirley stopped and turned her full attention to the younger woman. "Your landscaping choices should reflect who you are, not just the business. It's a reflection of the inner you."

"I didn't know you were into the psychological aspect of gardening," Maggie said, still surprised that the older woman seemed years younger since she started designing landscaping for the Tiny House Haven community where she lived. Not to mention the various friends and family in Percyville who had benefited from Shirley's keen eye and thrifty budgeting. While she hired out the actual heavy labour, the design and choices were all Shirley's imaginative concepts.

Shirley settled in, as if about to delve into her favourite topic. "I've been reading a lot of gardening magazines to keep up with the trends, and there's a young woman who writes a column about integrating a person's personality into their surroundings. It's quite interesting." She sat forward, once again all business, as she pulled out a pamphlet of various shrubs. "Now here are some ideas I had about – oh, wait, I drew a plan."

She pulled a hand-drawn page from the back of the folder and placed it on the table between them. "The yellow marks are what you have now, and the green are considerations."

Maggie took a minute to study the plan, well aware of Shirley's intense gaze. "What's that on the side of the building?"

Shirley lifted her head to look through her bifocals and tapped her finger on the red mark. "That's a climbing vine. My research indicates that a morning glory would be appropriate for your café. They grow fast and need pruning every year, but they have a beautiful blue flower that would accent your sign. I've always thought blue was your color. But that's just my opinion."

Maggie noticed the neat handwriting pointing out specific shrubs and flower beds. "This looks great, Shirley. There are so many choices and it's all amazing. And maybe we could do something to attract birds." Maggie took a breath and asked. "Will this be expensive?"

Shirley gathered up the papers and shoved them into the folder before pulling up her chair. "Leave that to me, young lady," she said brusquely, then gave Maggie one of her rare smiles. "I know just the place to get everything at a good price. I bring them a lot of business, and they like me there."

And with that she was gone, making sure the door didn't hit the wall this time, leaving Maggie shaking her head in wonder at the elderly whirlwind of a woman.

Alone again, her hand stole into her pocket. She slowly pulled out the crumpled envelope and placed it on the table in front of her, smoothing it with her fingers. She drank in the sight of her grandmother's loving handwritten greeting, almost afraid to open it.

***

Daphne burst through the front door, grinning as if Maggie had already won the first-place ribbon, and proudly displayed it in the café. "Maggie!" she called out as she got ready for her shift. "Everyone was so happy. They're all hoping you'll win and knock old Myrtle Smythe off her perch."

"Cool."

Daphne stopped short when she saw Maggie staring at the envelope. "I forgot to tell you. Sorry. Your notary, who is very handsome in an old-fashioned way, dropped that off and sampled a pastry. He loved it and asked me to tell you he's sorry he missed you."

Maggie stood and wrapped her fingers protectively around the envelope as she headed for the stairs to her living quarters above. "I'll be a few minutes."

"Take all the time you want," Daphne called after her. "It's pretty quiet..."

But Maggie was gone, up the narrow stairs to her home above, closing the door at the top behind her. She found comfort in the big chair by the back window and sat down with a plop. She passed the envelope back and forth from one hand to the other.

Maggie took a few deep breaths, gazed out at the Tiny House Haven beyond, and watched as the sun glistened off the lake around which it was built. It always amazed her how soothing nature was.

With a slow and even pressure, she slid her fingernail under the flap and pulled it back, letting the pages inside fall out into her lap. A scent of lilac wafted from them, and she lifted the pages to her nose and took a deep breath. She remembered that scent; her mother used to wear it.

She began to read, squinting to make out the writing.

"My dearest Marguerite, By now you must think me strange as I dole out information bit by bit in separate letters. But it's the only way I can do this, for both of us. I have so much to ask your forgiveness for. I hurt your mother in such a selfish way that she refused to allow me to have you in my life.

I was in love once, many years ago, during the war. We were in love, I should say. We were young. He swept me off my feet and then he was out of my life within a month.

Graham was your grandfather, Florence's father, and I let her believe that he had died in the war. Perhaps he had. His letters stopped abruptly, and I had no way of finding him. I was pregnant by then, and never told him. Then I was a single mother, pretending to be a widow, starting a business, struggling to survive.

I would change nothing, my little one, except that I never really knew you.

Your mother left when she found out about Graham, and I have no idea who told her. She railed at me that all these years she could have been looking for him. I only gave her his first name because I didn't want her to find him, only to find out he might want nothing to do with us. I was so ashamed of being pregnant out of wedlock. Although I pretended to everyone around me that I was married and now a widow, most people assumed the truth.

I received one letter from him and then nothing. After that, all my letters were returned without explanation. I suspected the worst.

Florence asked me why I never looked for him. My pride was very strong—I really believed that if he loved me, he would come back. When she asked if he knew I was pregnant, I had to say no. And then she asked me what reason he would have to come back at all. Shame and heartbreak are a terrible duo to fight.

Your mother left the next day, refusing to speak to me or answer my letters. But I kept my eyes open and saw her wedding announcement in the newspaper. Then, a year later, your birth announcement appeared. Oh, what joy, I thought! A granddaughter. I wrote to your mother, but she never replied.

By then, my business was doing very well. I was Boulangerie Tavie! It had taken years, and I poured my heart into this bakery to create something that I hoped would bring comfort and joy to those who tasted my desserts. I'm sure you've met Veronique and Samuel. They are perfect for the business, and I hope you will keep them. But I have no right to ask you for anything, do I?

I have followed your life as best I could. Notary Bouchard, Jean-Pierre, has always been a good friend and helped me. I found out where you went to school and secretly attended your high school graduation. I stayed in the back so that Florence would not see me. You were beautiful! I stopped by your Cozy Corner Café last year. I couldn't help myself! You probably don't remember me. I'm the lady who talked about the best way to blind bake a crust."

Maggie's mouth dropped open. She remembered this woman well. They had talked for an hour on a quiet autumn afternoon. They'd sat at a table, drinking tea, eating eclairs and laughing about the "tried and true" rules of baking, which were often tweaked at will to still produce a special crust. She had felt so comfortable with this complete stranger. But she had not been a stranger, she had been her own grandmother.

A tear trickled down her cheek. She brushed it away as she thought of what her mother had taken from her. Not just her, but also her grandmother.

She continued reading.

"*Then why did I not tell you who I was? Your mother had died, but I did not want to bring it all up and cause you more pain. Sometimes what we think is the best is not. But now I will end this letter because my hand hurts! My dear Marguerite, I wish you a wonderful life. May you find a young man to make your heart swell like my Graham did for me. I hope you fill your home with children and live long enough to hear the laughter of grandchildren.*

Forgive me. I did the best I could.

You will always be in my heart.

Much love, Octavie (grandmere)."

Maggie let the pages fall to her lap and sat staring out the window, seeing nothing, lost in the past, wondering what might have been.

Chapter Seventeen

Maggie gathered the teacups for Ellie's genealogy senior group and set them on the counter. She grinned as a boisterous laugh came from the back room. Lennie must be telling jokes again.

The front door to the cafe swung open and Maggie looked up to see Francois strut into the room. Her heart sank.

He paced around, checking things out, poking this, lifting that, pausing in front of the Bake Fair notice on the bulletin board as if it were an important document. He drew out the tension and took his time before stopping in front of her. He gave her a wide grin. Her stomach clenched and the telltale acid burn angered her. He had invaded her domain, and polluted it with his presence.

"Can I help you?" She turned to wash her hands at the sink, then grabbed a towel to wipe them down, creating more space between them.

"I think you can." His smile never reached his eyes, but it remained on his face as if to convince her. "I'll need some of my inheritance soon."

She pushed away from the counter and leaned toward him. The move caught him off guard and he shuffled back awkwardly. She kept her voice low so as not to disturb the seniors in the meeting room. He tilted his head to hear her.

"I'm tired of you demanding things I have no control over! Talk to Notary Bouchard and leave me alone."

With a burst of bravado, he puffed out his chest and pressed his face close to hers. She held her ground, refusing to move.

"I have some people I need to... help with a repayment." He held her gaze for a few seconds, but looked away first. "I need something now!" Despite his downward gaze, his words came fast and furious.

Maggie took a deep breath, trying to appear bored and hoping her fear didn't show. "Like I said, talk to..."

Phil rose from his seat at the genealogy table and took a step toward her. She shook her head and winked, as if to tell him everything was fine. But he stayed where he was, letting her know he was watching.

"I'll take a loan and pay you back."

"How much are you talking about?" Not that Maggie would give him anything, but she wanted to know how much he owed.

"Ten thousand should do it." He looked around the café again.

"I don't have that kind of money." Maggie turned away. "If you're not buying anything, you can leave now."

He hesitated, his eyes darting from side to side like a cornered animal. Then he stepped beside her and lowered his voice. "You have insurance on this place, right?"

At that moment Ellie strode into the cafe, having seen him from outside. "What are *you* doing here?"

Francois stepped back from Maggie and made his way around the fireball that was Ellie, her hands clenched as if waiting for an excuse to hit him. When he reached the door, he turned and waved. "Remember what I said."

Silence filled the building. Everyone had been watching the exchange. Phil slowly returned to his seat.

As Francois's car disappeared from view, Maggie slumped against the wall. Her shoulders shook as a tiny bead of sweat trickled down her spine.

"What the heck was that?" Ellie whispered, knowing that Maggie would not want her troubles broadcast to everyone in the café.

Maggie turned her back to the group and whispered. "He wants money from me, so I told him to talk to Notary Bouchard. End of story." She didn't want to burden her friend with this.

Ellie gave the seniors a quick glance, then returned to Maggie. "Don't worry, he's too chicken to do anything."

"I'll be back with your tea in a few minutes." Maggie walked away, jamming her fingers into her pockets to stop them shaking, worried Ellie might be wrong this time. Cornered animals often did crazy things.

***

Ellie dropped her briefcase on the large table and looked around at her group of seniors. After months of meetings, each of them had become friends, each with different reasons for choosing to learn how to write their memoirs.

"So, what are we going to learn today, dear?" Ruth asked.

"I need to talk to Maggie for a minute," Shirley announced abruptly, leaving the group with a flower magazine gripped in her hand, "business stuff." But they could all see her huddled with Maggie at the counter, voices lowered, Shirley's hand on Maggie's shoulder, magazine nowhere in sight.

"She's too busy for us now?" Lennie asked, getting a chiding nudge in the ribs from Tess.

"She's helping Maggie landscape the front of the Café," Ruth said, her pride in her sister's abilities obvious to all.

"Shirley finished my window boxes last week," Phil said. "They really brighten up the place." He stole a quick glance at the woman in question, sure that no one knew he had a crush on her. Of course they all knew—Phil was an open book—though they were too nice to tease him about it. Phil was a quiet man who liked his privacy. No doubt this sudden blossoming of affection for the brash and pushy Shirley had thrown him for a loop.

Norma caught his eye and smiled, obviously knowing where the wind was blowing with him and his interests. "I'll ask her to look over my garden when she gets a chance."

"Aunt Norma!" Ellie looked surprised. "Your garden is amazing. I really doubt you need any help."

"It wouldn't hurt to get a second opinion." Norma said. "And maybe I could get some ideas from her."

"Fair enough."

"Ellie, we talked about wills last time. Is there anything else you want to share?" Ruth asked. As a long-time teacher at the nearby high school, she had a knack for reading between the lines. Her memory and thought processes were exceptional for a woman in her nineties.

"Well..." Ellie wasn't sure what to say, but Maggie had overheard Ruth's question and hurried to the table with the pot of tea. Shirley also returned and took a seat next to her sister, giving the group her full attention.

Maggie said, "There is something else," and set the teapot down.

"Is there a problem?" Lennie asked, still curious about any legal matter.

"Notary Bouchard doesn't think so." Maggie said. "And that's good enough for me."

"Lennie," Ellie said, "just to be clear, if we put everything in a will, can anyone challenge it? Like demand proof of something because they don't agree with the will?"

"I suppose they can challenge or contest it, but from what Maggie told us before, if a notary drew up the will, I'm sure he crossed the T's and dotted the I's."

"I'm positive he did more than that." Maggie leaned against the table and considered his words. "I think he was in love with my grandmother, so I bet he made sure her wishes were exactly how she wanted."

"Oh, another love story," Doreen sighed, her knitting needles slowing for a second before resuming their rhythmic clicking.

"At least one," Ellie said before she realized everyone was looking her way, waiting for her to explain. "But for now, we'll dive into the Drouin records and see if we can find a birth or baptismal record for Maggie's mother."

"I thought you'd never get there," Maggie muttered as she pulled up a chair next to her.

Ellie opened her computer. "You've been extremely patient."

"I thought you'd walk in here with the document held high," Maggie said. "I'm the one who's surprised by *your* patience."

"I have to admit I almost did look for it," Ellie said sheepishly, "but I want to be surprised along with the rest of you."

"Don't you have your mother's birth certificate?" Shirley asked Maggie.

"My dad couldn't find it," Maggie said. "He'd never even seen one."

"So." Ellie turned her computer around so they could all see the screen. They gathered closer. Doreen dropped her knitting onto her lap. "I'll start by putting in Florence's name and date of birth."

"How did you get her date of birth?" Phil asked.

"We celebrated her birthday every year," Maggie smiled at him.

"Sorry." Phil shook his head and rolled his eyes.

"Phil," Ellie said, "never feel foolish for asking a question. I'm *still* asking them. Okay, here we go. Ancestry has two entries, one for a Flora Duprat, another for a Florence Duprat. The first one was born in Montreal; the other was born in St. Anne de Lafont."

"Bingo!" Maggie squinted at the computer. "What else does it say?"

"Hang on, let's open the file."

"Oh, my, it's in French and so small!" Norma said.

"Just give me a second." Ellie adjusted the computer. The record of Florence's baptism filled the screen. "Okay, let me translate. On the third day of November, 1946, the undersigned baptized Florence Duprat, daughter of Octavie Duprat, of this parish and Graham Brodie of Moose River, New Brunswick."

"Wait," said Shirley. "Isn't it supposed to say something like by the lawful marriage of the parents?"

Ellie checked with Maggie and waited for Maggie's nod of agreement before answering. "They weren't married. But this gives us Maggie's grandfather's last name and where he came from. Information we didn't have before."

"And now you have that direct line you've been looking for," Ruth reminded her.

"That's great." Maggie looked around at the faces of her elderly neighbours. "And it's about all the excitement I can take right now." They smiled as if they had solved their own mystery. "Eclairs for everyone!" She jumped out of her seat and went behind the counter to fill a tray with the delicious pastries.

"I hear you're entering the bake-off tomorrow," Lennie said to her, his eyes wide with anticipation as Maggie put the plate on the table. "Is this what you're entering?"

"Oh, no," Maggie grinned mischievously. "One of the things my grandmother left me were some new recipes. Did I mention she was Boulangerie Tavie?"

Everyone's mouths dropped open, and Phil pumped his arm in the air. "A new bake-off winner for sure!"

Chapter Eighteen

Maggie rose before the sun, dressed in her work clothes, and made her way down the dark stairwell to the café, her fingertips skimming along the wall.

The building felt peaceful until she broke the silence by grinding coffee beans and setting up a pot to get her through the next few hours. She realized that breakfast would be a smart idea, but she settled for a day-old oatmeal cookie and sipped her first cup of coffee while reading and rereading Octavie's recipe.

She had to do this right. Maggie wanted to show people that she was her grandmother's heir.

And with that thought running through her head, she stopped. Was this the truth? It sounded selfish, even to her own ears. She sat down at a table, cup and cookie in hand, and considered her motivation.

She'd never been one to show-off, but was that what she wanted? Was she just trying to show Myrtle Smythe that other people were just as good? And why did she have to be the conquering hero of Myrtle's downfall?

Truth be told, Myrtle wasn't a bad person, even though she regularly came into the café to make disparaging remarks about Maggie's apple pie to everyone in earshot. For, as every citizen of Percyville had been told by Myrtle, the only apple pie worth eating was her own.

No, Maggie's desire to win went deeper than outdoing old Myrtle Smythe. It stemmed from her feelings about her own worth as a baker. Customers raved about her baked goods, but for some reason, she never believed those words herself.

So this was all about proving it to herself.

Winning a first-place ribbon wouldn't solve that, but it could be a start, she told herself as she stretched and grabbed her grandmother's recipe from the table.

Soon the sounds of pots banging and jars opening filled the café. That and a little soft jazz in the background.

***

By the time Daphne arrived at half past six, all traces of baking had been washed and put away. A delicious aroma greeted her as she walked through the front door, and she stopped in her tracks.

"Oh, my goodness, what delight is that?" With her nose in the air, she followed the scent into the kitchen and spotted two pies on the immaculate counter.

Maggie sat next to them, her hair escaping from a bun to trail to her shoulders, apron stained, face smudged with flour, hands clenched tightly around a third cup of coffee. And she was smiling.

"Does it smell good?" she whispered, unwilling to shatter the spell she'd woven that morning, alone with the ghost of her grandmother and a weathered recipe card.

"Oh, Maggie." Daphne leaned in and took a deeper whiff of the pies. "I'd give an hour's pay for a bite of this."

Maggie ran for a knife, fork and plate and returned to cut a piece of one of the pies for her stunned employee. She shoved it into Daphne's hands. "I don't need your money, just your honest opinion."

Daphne took the fork and sliced off a generous portion. She lifted it to her nose again, then let it slip into her mouth and land on her tongue. She closed her eyes.

"Mmmm," she moaned. "This is so good!"

"Awesome!" Maggie cut two more pieces, placed them carefully into paper bags, and headed for the door. "Put the pies away and guard them with your life.

I'll be back in a flash." She paused before reaching the door. "Oh, and half the pastries for the day are done. The rest should be a snap."

Daphne watched her sprint across the road and disappear into the woods on the other side. She was taking her newest creation to Ellie.

***

Maggie slowed her gallop deep in the forest, afraid of tripping over a tree root and dropping the precious bags in her hand.

A slow, precise hammering coming from the barn drew her attention, and she headed there as she burst out of the woods.

The doors were wide open, and she watched as Quinn worked wooden pegs into the underside of a large chair. Cali sat at his feet, out of the way, but close enough to feel his warmth.

The dog saw her and bounded for the door, tail wagging, a crisp single bark announcing her presence. Maggie bent down and ran the fingers of one hand through her fur, the other hand holding the bags of pie above her head and away from Cali's curious nose.

"Hey!" Ellie came up behind her and gave her a quick hug. "You're up early. Getting ready to bake the winner?"

Quinn propped his tool on the bench and strolled over, his sense of smell as acute as Cali's had been. "I think she's already done that." The low morning sun lit up the inside of the barn, accentuating the scar he'd picked up as a police officer in Scotland. Maggie wondered if that was why he felt the need to work alone? Could her grandmother have felt the same, the need to be away from the prying eyes of her community, raising her child by herself?

Maggie dug into the bags and handed each of them a piece of pie. "Sorry, no plates or cutlery."

Ellie and Quinn bit into their slices at the same time, their eyes wide with surprise.

"Oh, this is..." Ellie took a second bite.

"Maybe I should add..." Maggie said.

"Nothing!" Ellie sputtered. "Absolutely nothing. This is the best pie I've ever tasted!"

"There's something in it I can't put my finger on," Quinn said.

"The secret ingredient." Maggie grinned, shuffling from one foot to the other. And then the next minute she collapsed, as if someone had let the air out of her balloon of excitement. She leaned against the barn door. "I didn't realize how much I wanted to win this!"

"Everybody wants you to beat Myrtle Smythe!" Ellie popped the last piece into her mouth and eyed the small morsel left in Quinn's hand.

"Don't even think about it!" He tossed it into his mouth and grinned at her, his cheeks stuffed but enjoying every crumb. "Sorry to rush you, but if I want to see Maggie win later, I have to finish this chair." He returned to his hammer and the commissioned piece of furniture that lay across the huge workbench in the middle of the barn. "And Maggie, that pie is exceptional."

"Okay, right." Maggie walked out the door, wiping her sweaty hands on her jeans. "I have to make it through the morning. I can do this."

"And we'll be there this afternoon to cheer you on," Ellie said as she walked with her through the woods to the highway, grabbing her hand and giving it a quick squeeze. "You'll be fine."

"Look at all the cars," Maggie whispered. The café parking lot was full, and it had only just opened.

"I guess people want to encourage you," Ellie said. "Go on, meet your audience."

"Don't jinx me, Ellie!" Maggie crossed her fingers against the jinx, checked the road for cars, then dashed across.

***

As Maggie walked into her crowded café, the noise level diminished as everyone saw her, then rose again as they all vied to wish her well in the competition. The tables were full of customers enjoying coffee and pastries. Even the table in the back was full.

"You're going to show her, aren't you, Maggie dear?" said Janice Smythe, Myrtle's sister. Maggie couldn't believe that Myrtle's own flesh and blood was rooting for her.

"Well, I…" Maggie tried to step past Janice, but the older woman grabbed her arm with claw-like fingers and held on tight.

"I mean, I love her and all, but she's so unbearable after a win. And it's about time the ribbon was passed on."

"We'll have to wait and see." Maggie pulled away and smiled at Janice as she went behind the counter and put her apron on. She could see that Daphne was flustered, but she had kept the flow of orders going while Maggie had been gone.

"Gosh," Daphne whispered to her as they stood at the sink washing their hands. "It's not like you were about to win the Nobel Peace Prize!"

"I haven't won anything yet." Maggie dried her hands and turned to the next customer. Her nerves sent tingling spikes across her skin as she faced a room full of people who believed victory was hers. If only she felt the same way.

The morning flew by. More and more people dropped in to offer support and encouragement, all vowing to come to the baking competition that afternoon. Every single item on the shelves was sold by the time the last person left and Maggie turned the sign on the door. The café was closed for the day.

Daphne collected dishes from the tables. "I can't remember ever selling out before lunch."

"Never!" said Maggie incredulously.

"You should enter baking competitions more often." Daphne stacked the dishwasher and hung up her apron. "I'll see you at the town hall at two. Make sure you eat something before you come. You look hungry." She gave Maggie a quick hug, grabbed her purse, and left.

Maggie hesitated, one hand fiddling with the knot on her apron She took in the quiet that never came at lunchtime in her café, marveled at the empty pastry shelves, and let a slow smile wash away her worry.

She could do this, she thought, and went upstairs to change.

She *would* do this.

Chapter Nineteen

A huge red tent greeted Maggie as she arrived at the town hall. Judging by the number of cars parked in the lot and all along the street, the sheer volume of people had to be the reason the event had been moved from inside to the grassy field across the road.

She stepped out of her car with her boxed pie as Ellie ran up and slid to a stop, her arms flailing with excitement. "You won't believe what's happening! When people found out you'd entered the contest, they told Mayor Savard they were coming this afternoon. His secretary barely managed to move the event outside in time."

"I can see that." Maggie looked at the brightly colored banners hanging from every available surface, and then at the tent, where several tables were already laden with baked goods.

"Come on." Ellie pulled her along. "I'll show you where your pie will be. Prime location."

Maggie felt out of place with everyone's eyes on her, people wishing her luck as they passed, some even patting her on the back and saying, "Go get her, Maggie."

"It's like they all want me to win," Maggie said in amazement.

"First of all, they love you." Ellie pulled her into the tent and over to a table that Quinn was leaning against. He was talking to two local tree farmers about buying wood for his business. "Second of all," Ellie said, giving Quinn a quick kiss on the cheek before continuing, "they want you to dethrone Myrtle!"

"Such pressure," Maggie muttered to herself, placing her pie behind her name tag. Myrtle's pie sat on a crystal pedestal a few feet away, as if claiming to the world that her baked goods were better than anyone else's. Next to them were two other entries, Karen Wallace, who entered year after year, in hopes of one day beating Shirley, and a young newcomer to the contest, Adele Prevost.

"Good luck to you all," said Karen softly to Maggie and Adele. Shirley was nowhere in sight. "One of us will win this year, I'm sure."

"I hear Myrtle never loses," Adele said, looking around as if the woman herself was standing there listening to them.

"Your pies are amazing, Karen," Maggie said. "And I'd love to try your baking, Adele."

"Well," Adele smiled, revealing a set of stainless-steel braces that gleamed in the sun, "we all agree we don't care who beats Myrtle, just that one of us does!"

Quinn's farmers moved on and Quinn gave Maggie's shoulder a gentle squeeze. "You'll be fine. From the gossip I hear, everyone is pulling for you."

Suddenly, the crowd around them parted to reveal a ruddy-faced Myrtle storming toward the table, dragging the hapless mayor in her wake. She planted herself in front of the table, towering over Maggie and her modestly displayed pie. Myrtle was a tall woman, large of frame, and loud. "I don't think this is fair!" Myrtle bellowed. She turned to the mayor to make sure she had his attention, then gazed out over the crowd to check that her complaint had reached them. "Maggie is a professional baker, which gives her an unfair advantage!"

Mayor Savard pulled his arm from her firm grip and gave Maggie an apologetic smile. "There's no rule against it, Myrtle, and you know that. Maggie is more than welcome to participate, and I can't wait to taste her pie, win or lose." He took a quick peek at Maggie's pie, licked his lips, nodded to everyone, and hurried off.

Janice Smythe approached her sister cautiously, knowing how upset Myrtle had been to learn that Maggie had entered the contest. "Come on, Myrtle, let's mingle before they judge the other entries." She tried to pull her sister behind her, but Myrtle stood her ground and glared at Maggie.

"Mark my words, young lady," Myrtle practically spat, "there's no chance you'll beat me. No one ever does. My pies are the best!"

Janice grabbed Myrtle's arm and maneuvered her through the crowd.

"Oh, yeah," Ellie said under her breath, "I should tell you that Janice is one of the judges."

***

Maggie and Ellie spent the next hour walking around, admiring the baked goods for sale that were entered in other category events. Quinn bought too many cookies, and since Maggie and Ellie were too nervous, he ate most of them.

Cheers erupted for the winners of the other categories, and as each of the bake-off tables emptied from the sales, the crowd eagerly moved on to the main event—the reason so many had come. The finale—the pie tasting competition. People found space wherever they could, in the aisles, on crates in the back, even spilling out from under the shade of the massive tent.

The mayor strode up to the table as Maggie, Myrtle, Karen and Adele took their places behind their respective pies. Myrtle held a knife with a long red ribbon attached to it and took three antique plates from her large bag, and set everything out in front of them.

Maggie motioned frantically to Ellie. "I've got nothing to put my pieces on!" she whispered.

Ellie dashed off, returning seconds later with plates, forks and a knife, handed to her by other fair contestants who were eager to lend a hand.

"Here you go." Ellie set the items down beside Maggie and gave Myrtle a sunny smile in return for the older woman's sneer.

"Please, allow me," Myrtle said in a sweet voice. She cut and plated three slices of her pie, handing the first to the mayor, the second to her sister, and the third to an elderly gentleman she batted eyes at.

"Sweet Marie," Maggie muttered, "she's flirting with a judge!"

The older gentleman plunged his fork into the pie and popped a small morsel into his mouth. His eyes closed, and he seemed to swirl the pie around in his mouth, like a first sip of wine.

Maggie and Ellie looked at each other, trying and failing to suppress grins at the man's theatrics.

"Oh, divine, my dear," said the older man. "Simply divine, as usual."

"Oh, Harold," Myrtle smiled, "you're too kind."

Janice took a bite and chewed as if it were a chore, smiling as her sister stared at her with narrowed eyes. "Nice," was all she said.

Mayor Savard then took a large piece of pie and chewed it, making mmm sounds and nodding his head. "Once again, very lovely indeed, Myrtle."

Myrtle preened at the compliments and sent a smile out to the crowd, sure of her place in the competition.

Karen held out her pie for tasting, and each judge kept a poker face, though Janice took an extra bite and winked at Karen.

As Adele passed pieces of her pie to the judges, Myrtle snorted as she looked at it. It was lopsided and slightly dark on one side. "It's my first attempt," Adele said with a big smile. The judges were kind, but no one took a second bite of her pie.

"And now we'll have a taste of Maggie's entry," Mayor Savard said as he turned to her.

Maggie cut three pieces and gave each judge a plate. She almost dropped the plate for the Mayor as her hands were slippery with sweat. Once everyone's eyes were off her, she wiped them on her pants.

Harold took a bite and chewed quickly, as if trying to get something horrible out of his mouth. As he prepared to swallow, he stole a quick sideways glance at Maggie, as if in surprise. Myrtle watched him like a hawk. "So, Harold," she prodded him, "what do you think?"

He took a minute, which seemed like hours to Maggie, and finally gave his opinion. "Very nice." Myrtle seemed satisfied and nodded to him, smiling and fluttering her eyes again.

Ellie turned away from the table so Myrtle and Harold wouldn't see her grin. She closed her eyes tightly and willed herself not to laugh out loud. When she regained control, she turned back as the mayor shoved a large piece of Maggie's pie into his mouth.

"Oh, my," he said before he had finished chewing. His eyes were wide with delight and he savored the bite before speaking. "Sorry about that. My parents raised me better than to talk with my mouth full. That was extraordinary, Maggie. Well done."

Out of the corner of her eye, Maggie caught Harold nodding his head in agreement before going still as Myrtle's gaze shifted to him.

The crowd waited breathlessly as Janice took a bite. She knew the game. She could keep a straight face and not reveal whether she enjoyed the morsel or not. "Very nice."

"And now," the mayor said with a flourish, "if you will excuse us, we will step outside and make our decision. Won't take a moment."

"I'm sure it won't," Myrtle said loudly as the three judges walked between the onlookers and disappeared.

Karen and Adele winked at each other, as if sure they had no chance, then gave Maggie a gentle nudge and nod, as if to say, well done, now we have a contest.

Conversation resumed in the crowd and people shouted out their good wishes for Maggie. Not one person looked at Myrtle. Her smile faded, then shot to supernova brightness as the judges returned within minutes.

The mayor looked surprised but happy. Janice refused to look at her sister, and Harold stared at the floor.

Ellie grabbed Maggie's hand for support but had to adjust the finger-crunching grip. "Easy, Mags," she whispered.

Once again, the crowd fell silent. Myrtle's gaze bored into the mayor, not looking left or right.

"By unanimous vote," the mayor began. Folding her large hands modestly over her ample belly, Myrtle smiled and looked around to make sure everyone was paying attention to her. Mayor Savard's voice rose, "We declare Maggie Williams the winner! Congratulations Maggie!"

"Wait, what?" Myrtle looked at her sister pleadingly. "What do you mean, Maggie wins?"

"I'm sorry, Myrtle," Janice said, though she sounded anything but sorry. "Maggie's pie had that little something extra that made it spectacular."

"But, but..." Myrtle stammered, reaching for the first-place ribbon the mayor handed to Maggie.

"Well done," he said, shaking Maggie's hand.

"But..." Myrtle turned to see Harold walking away, his plate with Maggie's piece of pie in hand.

Karen and Adele gave Maggie a huge hug. "We knew someone would dethrone her eventually!" Karen said.

"Speech, speech," called an anonymous voice from the crowd.

"Oh, my goodness," Maggie stammered. "What can I say except thank you so much. This is such a surprise."

"It shouldn't be," Ellie said in a voice loud enough so everybody could hear. "Everyone knows Maggie is a brilliant baker."

"But she's a professional!" whined Myrtle, still standing beside the remains of her pie.

"She's only a professional because she sells her goods," Janice said. "If you sold your pies, you'd be a professional too!" And with that, she walked away.

"Will you be serving the winning pie at the Café anytime soon?" a voice called from the back.

"Why yes," Maggie said. "Starting next week!"

Myrtle fumed as everyone came to congratulate Maggie, her face a mottled shade of pink. In a huff, she grabbed her bag, scraped the pie off the plates and put them and the pedestal inside. She left her pie on the table and eased her way out of the crowd.

Ellie watched her go, sympathetic enough to feel pity for the older woman. As Myrtle reached the edge of the crowd, Ellie glimpsed a man in the distance, staring at the tent. And then he was gone.

Her concern for Maggie made her see Francois everywhere.

***

Maggie, Ellie, and Quinn returned to the empty café and applauded as Maggie hung her first-place ribbon on the wall by the front door.

"Is it too flashy?" She frowned.

"Not at all," Quinn said, standing back and admiring the placement. "It adds the perfect touch of color to the room."

"I wish Pete could have been here," Maggie said.

"When is he getting back?" Ellie asked.

Maggie leaned against the counter and smiled. "In a couple of days. Once this project is finished, he said he won't be doing any jobs away from home. At least not for a while."

"He's a good cousin, and I knew he'd make you a wonderful boyfriend." Ellie grinned.

"Boyfriend!" Maggie scoffed. "Ellie, we're not teenagers anymore. Do you call Quinn your boyfriend?"

Ellie turned to Quinn and caught his wide-eyed look of surprise. 'I..."

"Indeed, I am," he assured her, wrapping his arm around Ellie's shoulders and planting a deep kiss on her lips. "But this boyfriend has to get back to work."

"And the final edits of my book awaits." Ellie took Quinn's hand and kept his arm around her shoulders. "So, we'll bid you adieu, Percyville Bake Sale First Place Pie Winner, and let you enjoy some quiet time."

Maggie walked them to the door. They put on helmets and climbed onto Quinn's motorcycle. Using Ellie's barn to build his large pieces of furniture, and moving into a spare room in her farmhouse, had clearly made Ellie happy again. All Maggie had ever wanted was to see her friend's sparkle return.

As the motorcycle drove away, Shirley pulled up and eased herself out of her car. "I heard you won! Thank goodness there's a new baking queen in town."

"Lucky, I guess," Maggie replied.

"I doubt that very much." Shirley strolled to the back of her SUV and opened the hatch. "I thought it was fixed from the start. You can't have a sister as a judge and have a fair fight."

"It was a unanimous vote," Maggie said.

Shirley turned to her in shock. "Janice voted against Myrtle?"

Maggie nodded.

"Well, I'll be." Shirley smiled. "There's hope for her yet. Now, come here, I've got a few samples and more photos. And then we'll go in for a slice of that winning pie and see that first-place ribbon."

Chapter Twenty

It was dinner time when Maggie finally closed the door behind Shirley and locked the café. She turned off the downstairs lights and made her way upstairs.

Leftovers were in order. She leaned against the counter as a butterfly pasta with meatballs warmed up in the microwave. The ding startled her out of her thoughts and she removed the plate.

So much to think about.

But first she'd take a few minutes to enjoy her victory in private. She did a solo fist pump in the air. "Well done, you!" she said aloud. As the words echoed off the walls, she again wished Pete was here with her. Even though they'd only been together for a short time, she knew what he would have done to celebrate: taken her out to dinner, opened a bottle of wine, finished said bottle of wine, then headed out into the woods for a night walk.

She could get used to having someone in her life.

Which brought her back to her grandmother. Maggie wondered how Octavie had managed after Graham had left, after she had found out she was pregnant. Raising a child alone was never easy, no matter what decade you lived in.

Maggie finished her meal, then grabbed her grandmother's scrapbook from the table and sank onto the couch to look through the various pictures again. Looking into someone's eyes in a photo, seeing a smile, made the people seem more real to her.

A sudden flash of headlights illuminated the inside of her apartment. She looked up, surprised that darkness had fallen. A car door slammed. Surely they could tell she was closed, she thought as she went to the window.

A gunshot shattered the silence. She jumped in surprise before dashing downstairs. The sound of breaking glass on the main floor and a car screeching away greeted her as she entered the Café.

The front window was shattered, the carpet below burning. Flames licked near to a display case, and smoke billowed as detectors went off one by one throughout the building. Maggie grabbed a bucket of melted ice and threw it on the flames. She ran to the fire extinguisher near the counter and emptied it onto the carpet and surrounding area until the fire was out.

Her eyes burned from the smoke, and a gut-wrenching fear gripped her, choking the air from her lungs. She raced around, opening all the windows to let the smoke out as the detectors continued to blare. Within minutes, a fire truck pulled into her parking lot, lights flashing, and two men ran to the front door.

Maggie struggled to unlock it before they broke it down. The latch clicked back and she swung the door open wide, gripping the handle for support, her legs suddenly unsteady, grateful for a lungful of cool, fresh air. "It's okay, it's okay!" she croaked. "I put it out, just a lot of smoke."

"Maggie!" Brian, the volunteer fire chief, grabbed her arm and pulled her out. "Great, but we need to check the whole place. Okay?" He led her to the bench, eased her onto it, and motioned for the other firefighter to stay with her.

"Hey, Derek," Maggie said to the young man. "Sorry about this."

"We were doing our monthly equipment verification when the call came in. What happened?" Derek asked, exchanging a nod with Brian, who disappeared into the cafe.

"Somebody threw something through the window!" She turned to him, still in shock, shaking her head in disbelief. "Why would someone do that? And there was a gunshot. What the hell is going on?"

The blaring of the smoke detectors faded one by one until silence engulfed them. Brian returned, a glass bottle covered in fire extinguisher goo in his gloved hand. "Looks like an amateur attempt at a Molotov cocktail."

A provincial police car pulled into the parking lot and a young female officer joined them. "Hey, guys, Maggie. What's going on?" she stared at the object in Brian's hand.

"Hey, Del. Got a call from someone who drove by, there was a fire here, smoke billowing and alarms going off."

"Were they able to identify the car that pulled out?" Maggie asked, nodding a hello to Del.

"They didn't mention any," Brian said. "Everything's fine here. Fire's out, not too much damage, mostly smoke and water. I'll write up the report when I get back to the station."

"Sounds good," Del said. She took a plastic bag from her belt and Brian dropped the evidence into it before taking his gloves off. Del sealed the bag tightly and wrote something on it.

"Thanks, guys." Maggie stood and shook their hands.

"Your instincts were excellent, Maggie," Brian said. "You did everything right. It could have been a lot worse." He patted her on the shoulder and he and Derek headed for the truck, but he stopped halfway. "And congratulations on beating Myrtle!"

"Thanks." Maggie gave a small smile, realizing that winning a blue ribbon meant nothing compared to almost losing her business.

As the fire truck pulled away, Del pulled out her notebook. "So, tell me what happened."

"You want to do this inside?" Maggie asked.

"Here's fine." Del moved to the bench. They sat side by side, their backs against the building.

"First I heard what sounded like a gunshot. No, before that, car headlights lit up the parking lot, *then* the shot."

"Were you open for business?"

"No." Maggie frowned. "I've been closed since noon for the Bake Fair."

"Congratulations on that," Del said. "Myrtle must have been upset."

"Maybe. I didn't see her leave."

"Well, it could have been someone who didn't know you were closed. Not from around here."

"But all the lights were out." Maggie fidgeted in her seat. "I mean the apartment lights were on, but the café was dark."

The sound of running feet startled them as Ellie and Quinn dashed across the highway.

"We heard the fire trucks," Ellie gasped. "What happened?"

Quinn ran to the front of the building.

"Don't touch anything," Del called after him.

"Not a thing," he assured her.

"To recap," Maggie said, for Ellie's benefit. "Someone drove into the parking lot, I heard a gunshot, and then they threw a Molotov cocktail through the window."

"What the hell?" Ellie yelled. "Are you kidding me?"

"They broke your camera," Quinn said when he returned.

Del went over and took some pictures of the camera and the front window. "Looks like the shot took out your surveillance camera."

"Who would...." Maggie caught Ellie's eye. They both had the same idea.

"Francois?" Ellie whispered.

"Who's Francois?" Del asked.

"I just inherited something from my grandmother, and he's also named in the will," Maggie said.

"Something!" Ellie laughed. "Something is she's the owner of the Tavie Bakery now!"

Del's eyes opened wide, and she nodded in appreciation. "Wow. Tavie was your grandmother?"

"Apparently," Maggie said.

"And this Francois?"

"He thought he was getting everything. He's like a cousin or something," Maggie said.

Ellie shook her head and muttered, "Cousin or something."

"Whatever." Maggie narrowed her eyes. "He wants his share now, and he thinks I can give it to him. The last time he was here, he asked me if I had insurance on the cafe."

"And I'm not sure, but I thought I saw him at the bake fair today." Ellie added. "But I could be wrong."

"Right." Del turned a page in her book. "His full name and address, phone number."

"I don't know." Maggie frowned, realizing she had no way of contacting him.

"But Notary Bouchard, of Bouchard and Champagne in Montreal, would," Ellie said.

"Okay." Del wrote it down, then put her notebook away. "As Brian said, it could have been worse."

"What if he comes back?" Maggie whispered, a sudden chill sending shivers down her body.

"I'll ask for more patrols tonight," Del said. "And tomorrow I'll call Notary Bouchard and that Francois guy and see what's going on."

"Thanks, Del," Ellie said. The young officer waved at her and headed back to her car and left.

"I'm going to get some wood from the barn and cover the front window," Quinn said. Maggie ran into his arms and hugged him tightly, then threw out an arm to pull Ellie into a group hug.

"I can't thank you guys enough," she mumbled before pulling away and taking a few deep breaths.

"Back soon." Quinn crossed the highway and disappeared into the woods.

"Okay," Ellie said, straightening her shoulders and clapping her hands. "Let's go in and see what we can do."

***

Ellie got the trash can, broom and dustpan, and work gloves from the kitchen. Together they carefully removed the remaining glass from the front window and swept up everything that was shattered in the water and foam on the floor. Ellie stole glances at her friend, worried by Maggie's silence. "Hey, maybe it was Myrtle," she joked.

"What?" Maggie looked up, startled from her thoughts.

"Ah, Mags." Ellie put the last piece of glass into the can and reached out for her friend.

Maggie collapsed against her, and even though she fought it, tears flowed. Her whole body shook as she let the shock work its way through her. She pulled away when the worst of the crying subsided, but held on tightly to Ellie's hands. "I couldn't bear to lose this place. I worked hard for it."

"I know," Ellie said. "Del will find Francois and..."

"What if it wasn't him?"

"Who else would have a reason to hurt you?" Ellie waited a minute for her to answer, but she didn't. "Right. No one."

Quinn's truck pulled up to the now gaping window, and he pulled a huge piece of plywood out of the back. He waved at them through the opening and hammered the sheet into place. "We'll have you closed up tight in a second, Maggie." All the light from outside faded as the wood sealed the space.

He came into the café and surveyed the damage.

"It's not as bad as I thought," Ellie told him, trying to lift Maggie's spirits at the same time.

"Do you want me to take the rug outside?" he asked.

Seeing the smoke and water staining it, Maggie nodded. "Please, thank you."

As he rolled it up and carried it out, Ellie filled another bucket with warm soapy water and washed down the wall around the broken window. The liquid got dirty, and she refilled it twice more before she was satisfied everything was clean.

Maggie wiped the floor, sweeping and washing until there was no trace of the damage. The fire itself had left no marks, thanks to her quick thinking, except for a slight burn on the rug.

Quinn helped move the furniture back into place, and Ellie washed out the bucket.

The silence between them had been bonding, soothing.

"Okay." Maggie surveyed the room and sniffed. "Better. Much better."

"The rug needs a good cleaning," Quinn said. "I rinsed it twice, but you're going to need a machine to do a deep wash."

"Thanks, guys."

"Shall I stay with you?" Ellie asked.

"No, no." Maggie waved her off. "I'll be fine. Del said she'd be patrolling more tonight, and I doubt he'll be back."

"Are you sure?" Ellie asked.

"Positive." Maggie smiled at her. "And you know what else I'm sure of? I understand exactly how Veronique and Samuel feel about losing the Tavie Bakery. They love that place as much as I love my café. I'm going to sell it to them."

Chapter Twenty-One

The next morning, as Maggie was taking the last tray of baked goods from the oven, she heard a car pull up with a quick honk. She stepped out to see Shirley throw open her door and ease out as a young lady hopped out of the passenger side and opened the trunk.

"I'll be right there," Maggie called. Shirley gave a quick nod without looking in her direction.

Maggie turned off the stove, then ran outside to find Shirley standing in front of the broken window.

"We heard the commotion last night but figured everything was okay when the noise stopped." Shirley glanced around, as if searching for the culprit. "What happened?"

Maggie filled her in with a condensed version of the story as they walked back to the car. Shirley listened intently, keeping her opinions to herself. "As long as you're okay, and the café didn't burn down, all is well, right?"

"I guess so," Maggie said, not quite believing it.

"And this is Julie," Shirley introduced her. "I hired her a while ago. She'll be performing the heavy lifting."

"I'm an intern, actually," Julie said, giving Shirley a bright smile. "I'm blown away by Miss Cooper's ideas and designs, and I can't wait to learn from her."

Maggie raised an eyebrow at the "Miss Cooper" reference and caught Shirley hiding a smile.

"We'll pot the plants by the entrance, set up the window boxes and fill them." Shirley went to the trunk. "And I have just the place for this."

Maggie followed her as Shirley pulled out a birdhouse replica of the Cozy Corner Café. It even included the fresh sign above the front door. Julie quickly reached out to catch it before it fell to the ground. "Thank you, dear," Shirley said.

"Oh, Shirley!" Maggie took it from Julie and ran her hands over the roof shingles, turning the miniature building around and noting all the little details. "Did you ask Quinn to do this?"

"He was happy to, and it's undoubtedly the icing on the cake for the whole upgrade."

"We'll need to find the perfect place for it," Maggie said.

"Once the last of the benches are in over by the woods, that would be an excellent spot. The birds will find it, and whoever sits there can enjoy them, too."

Maggie set the birdhouse on the ground and gave Shirley a huge hug. The older woman was not known for showing affection freely, but she patted Maggie's shoulder awkwardly before stepping back.

"So, I hope to get most of this in and done before the crowds arrive," Shirley said.

"Oh, not a problem," Maggie assured her. "I don't open for a while and it'll probably be a slow—"

The first car of the day pulled into the parking lot, followed by two more.

***

By ten that morning, Maggie had explained the fire to nearly thirty people, and sold most of her pastries. Daphne was in the back, baking small batches of every treat to get them through the rest of the day.

When Notary Bouchard walked in at eleven, the café was almost empty. He took one look at the boarded-up window and made a beeline for Maggie.

"Notary Bouchard." Maggie was delighted. "It's so good to see you."

He took her hand and gave it a warm squeeze, an old-fashioned mix of handshake and cupping that Maggie found comforting.

"I came as soon as I spoke to the officer about what happened last night."

"Please, sit down." Maggie motioned him to a table and joined him. "Can I get you anything?"

He looked at the display case and the fresh eclairs Daphne had laid out. Maggie nodded to her and held up two fingers. Within minutes, Daphne arrived with two eclairs and a pot of coffee.

Maggie turned the cups over and poured for them both. She handed one to Notary Bouchard, and pushed the sugar and milk containers in his direction, preferring to drink hers black. He gestured that he enjoyed it the same, but he took a bite of the éclair and closed his eyes in delight. Maggie smiled.

He sat back and cradled the cup in his hands. "So, tell me what happened last night. From the beginning."

Maggie told the story once again, filling in all the details she'd left out of the version she'd told the curious townspeople.

"He had some nerve to ask if you had insurance." Notary Bouchard shook his head. He wiped his fingers on a napkin and leaned toward her on the table. "I like the sound of that officer, and I have no doubt she'll find him. I've been trying to contact him since yesterday, but he never answers."

"That seems odd," Maggie frowned. "He's so desperate to get his inheritance, you'd think he'd jump when you called."

He gestured to the ribbon on the wall. "I see congratulations are in order."

"Spur of the moment thing." She waved her hand as if it was nothing. "I feel like I cheated because I used the recipe my grandmother left me. Oh, wait." She jumped out of her chair and ran to the back room, returning with the letter Octavie had written her. She handed it to him. "Will this hold up in court? Francois keeps saying he'll challenge who I am."

He pulled out his glasses and read it, smiling in certain places. "I doubt there will be any problems with your inheritance, Maggie. Octavie was very specific in her wording and clarification of how she wanted her estate to be handled. You don't have to prove you're an heir."

Maggie took the letter back and folded it carefully. "I guess I need confirmation for myself, as well. I never heard about Graham, or anything. Mom never talked about her family. It was like Mom just turned up one day out of the blue!"

"I guess this proves who your grandfather was, and how much Octavie loved you."

Maggie looked at the letter and then at Notary Bouchard. "I have decided to sell the bakery to Veronique and Samuel. They can pay over time and it will be a reasonable price. I know what it's like to start a business. But I'll keep a percentage, though they'll have majority control. I don't think my grandmother would want me to sell everything." She said the last part quietly, ashamed of appearing greedy.

He nodded. "Your grandmother would be thrilled to hear that. She had faith in this young couple to carry on her life's work. Especially since she knew you had your own path to follow here with the cafe."

"Would you take care of the paperwork for me? I'll go back there this afternoon and tell them myself."

"I'd be honored." He glanced at his watch, stood, and slid his chair under the table. "And now my playing hooky is over, and I must return to the office. I enjoyed the ride up here very much."

He gave her a quick double cheek kiss goodbye and left.

As his car pulled away, Maggie picked up her phone and dialed. "Ellie? How about another road trip?"

Chapter Twenty-Two

Ellie arrived after lunch and tossed her overnight bag into the back of Maggie's car before hopping into the passenger seat. She rolled down the window and waited. She drummed her fingers on the door and gazed up at the sky; not a cloud in sight. Perfect road trip weather.

Within minutes Maggie was throwing her own bag next to Ellie's and sliding behind the wheel, paper bag in hand. "Here, keep these safe, which means don't eat them now. We'll need them later."

Ellie peeked inside, and the aroma of freshly baked chocolate chip cookies wafted out. "Oh, jeez, Maggie, can I have one now, while they're still warm?"

Maggie pulled onto the highway, heading for St. Anne de Lafont. She glanced at her friend and grinned. "Only one. If you start eating them like chips, I'll never get any!"

Ellie took small bites to make the her allotted cookie last longer, then made a show of closing the bag and placing it at her feet. "Fill me in. Why the sudden rush to Grandma's house?" She turned and stifled a laugh. "Sorry, I didn't mean it to sound like that."

"What, a fairy tale?" Maggie lifted her sunglasses from the rear-view mirror and put them on. "I think we've established that this whole thing is exactly that, right?"

"Any news?"

"Notary Bouchard came by this morning."

"Oh?" Ellie sat up straighter, giving Maggie her full attention.

"Del called him and told him what had happened." Maggie eased the car onto the main highway and settled into a comfortable speed. "He tried to reach Francois as well, but couldn't."

"I'm pretty sure we know where he was last night!"

"He's confident that Del will find him, so that's a bit of a relief."

"A bit of relief is not completely though, right?"

Maggie frowned and shook her head. "I'm going to tell Veronique and Samuel that I'm selling them the bakery."

"Oh boy!" Ellie raised an eyebrow. "You're really giving it all away? I thought you were joking."

"Not all. Just the building, the name, and the recipes. They'll be the majority shareholders, but I'll keep a good share for myself."

"So, like a business deal where you keep a cut."

"Exactly." Maggie noticed Ellie's reticence. "I can't sell everything my grandmother built, and I don't think she'd want me to. But she cared about Veronique and Samuel, and I want to do this for them. *And* keep some for myself."

"Nobody said you were stupid."

"It's not about being smart *or* greedy." Maggie took another glance at the road behind her, enjoying having the road to themselves at this time of day. "It's about holding on to something I never knew I had, especially if it might help me learn more about my grandmother."

"Sounds like a good idea." Ellie gave her seal of approval.

Maggie changed the subject, needing to take her mind off things for a while. "Quinn seemed a little tired last night. Are you keeping him up late?"

"I wish," Ellie said with a grin. "He's got a big commission job for a new hotel. They want an exclusive reception area, and they thought his ideas were unique and edgy."

"What the heck does that mean?"

"No idea, but he's happy."

"Did he tell you he built me a birdhouse replica of the café?"

“No.” Ellie turned to her. “Boy, that guy sure keeps things close to his chest.”

“Except for how he feels about you.”

“Yeah, well, I doubt I’m much better.”

For the next hour they listened to music and sang along, talked in fits and starts about important thoughts and utter nonsense, sometimes shared the ride in silence, and ate the cookies.

“Grandma’s or the bakery?” Ellie asked as they crossed the small bridge leading into St. Anne de Lafont mid-afternoon.

“Grandma’s,” Maggie said as she turned onto the road past the church. “We’ll go to the bakery first thing in the morning.”

They pulled into the driveway and got their bags out of the back. Maggie closed the door and leaned against the car, eyes closed, face raised to the sun. “I love this, Ellie.”

Ellie watched her friend bask in the warmth of the sun and tranquility of the homestead, marveling once again at all that Maggie had inherited. It was quite impressive. Her gaze skidded to a stop when she noticed the front door open, swaying in the breeze.

“Maggie?” Ellie started for the front porch, but Maggie had seen the door and ran ahead. “Wait, maybe we shouldn’t go in.”

But Maggie raced through the door and into the chaos beyond. She took a shaky breath. “What the...”

The living room looked like it had been hit by a tornado. The quaint chairs lay on their sides, the lamp on the end table was broken on the floor. Every cushion on the couch was torn, and the glass figurines in the curio cabinet were shattered. The drawers in the rolltop were open, their papers strewn about.

Ellie walked around slowly. “Watch where you step.”

Maggie took it all in, from one side of the room to the other. “What the heck happened?” She followed Ellie’s footsteps, straightening furniture and avoiding glass.

"We need to check the rest of the house," Ellie said as Maggie grabbed a broom and started sweeping up the mess as best as she could.

"And the cabin!" Maggie's eyes widened in fear. "What if they destroyed the cabin, too?"

"Can you tell if anything's missing?"

Maggie shook her head. "I'm not sure. Wait, the old clock is gone and so are the silver candlesticks."

"There are empty spaces here," Ellie pointed at the cabinet. "Anything expensive?"

"I'm not sure." Maggie's heart ached, a physical pain running through her body. This was her grandmother's home; her grandmother's life was in this house. Someone had tried to destroy it. "Come on, I have to check the cabin."

It took them only a few minutes to run across the field, over the bridge and to the porch, only to be confronted with another open door.

Maggie slid to a stop, afraid to go inside. Ellie waited.

When Maggie finally stepped through the door, the damage didn't seem as bad as in the main house, though cushions and blankets were tossed around, and the few plates and cups were smashed on the floor. As Ellie started to get the broom, Maggie grabbed her by the arm.

"The scrapbook is gone." She pointed to the table, her hand shaking. "I left it here because I wanted to come back and study it in this cabin, in the place that meant so much to her."

"Are you sure?" Ellie moved things around, checking under the bed, behind the couch. Nothing.

"Graham's pipe is gone too," Maggie whispered. The tears she had fought so hard to keep at bay dripped onto her eyelashes, lingering there as if waiting to be released.

"Come on." Ellie grabbed her hand and led her outside. She shut the door tight behind her, but had no way of locking it. "We'll check the house and come back here later."

As they rounded the corner of the house, they noticed a police car parked behind Maggie's car. Maggie's heart sank with fear and her heart skipped a beat. What more could go wrong?

"Marguerite Williams?" asked the officer as he walked up to them. He was tall and thin, an attempt at growing a beard showed his young age.

"Yes." Maggie didn't move, afraid of what he would say.

"And you have a cousin," he consulted his notes, "Francois Duprat?"

"Yes." She dragged out the word.

"I'm sorry to tell you that he was in a car accident this morning."

"Is he okay?" Ellie asked.

"I'm sorry, no, he died from his injuries."

Maggie took a deep breath and slumped against her car. "What happened?"

The officer looked down at his notes and continued. "My great-aunt, Mrs. Ethier, lives right over there." He pointed to the small house by the church. "She called us this morning and said she had seen Mr. Duprat go into your house and leave with a box. She knew he had no right to do that, and on my way here, I came across the car accident."

"Whatever was in the box, he stole them." Ellie said, knowing she sounded shallow for not asking more about Francois.

"I have the items from his car." The officer pulled a box from the back seat and handed it to Maggie. "You want me to file a report?"

"What's the point?" Maggie opened the box and looked inside. There were the candlesticks and the edge of the scrapbook. "No, no, it's okay. I suppose you'll be contacting Francois's family? I just found out he was a relative, and I didn't know him and..."

"We notified them."

"Well, then," Ellie said as Maggie rifled through the box and found more items. "I guess that's about it. Thank you for bringing these things back. They mean a lot to her."

"Your grandmother was a wonderful woman," the officer said as he walked back to his car. "She's going to be missed."

Maggie turned to him, surprised to feel a small smile form on her lips. "Thanks. I'm sure she will."

***

Maggie made it into the house before collapsing on the couch, still clutching the box. "I can't believe this!"

"Let me." Ellie took the box from her and placed it on the kitchen table.

"Okay." Maggie jumped right back up, as if her nervous system wouldn't let her rest. "I need to get things back in order."

Ellie knew better than to push, and for the next while they went through the rest of the house, only to discover that Francois had focused his theft on the living room, leaving the rest of the house untouched. The destruction he had caused would have been equal to the items he had taken.

Ellie had taken a quick drive into town to buy new locks for the cabin and farmhouse, and was glad that when supper rolled around, it was quick and easy, basically whatever was left in the fridge. Maggie had known she'd be back soon and was glad she hadn't taken the food home the last time they were here.

Ellie finished her meal and tried to catch Maggie's eye. "Do you want to talk about it?"

"About what?" Maggie refused to lift her head.

"Francois."

The silence lasted a few minutes before Ellie reached for her friend's hand. "You're freezing! You need mittens!" Ellie tried to rub the warmth back into Maggie's fingers. Maggie sat still, accepting the comfort, but not speaking.

"Okay." Ellie stopped rubbing and held Maggie's hands gently, keeping a quiet connection between them. "The last few hours of chatting have been wonderful, the silences not so much. Let's talk about this. You do know that none of his problems were because of you?"

"Why would I think they were?"

"Because that's who you are, you take everything on your shoulders."

Maggie pulled up, detaching their hands and hiding hers on her lap under the table. "Well, I don't." She gave Ellie a hard look. "I don't feel responsible at all. In fact, I'm super ticked off about the whole thing."

"Maggie..."

Maggie held up a hand to stop her. "Let me finish. I'm angry that we've both been put in this position. Who knows what kind of person Octavie was. Maybe she led Francois on, telling him he'd inherit everything."

"And maybe she was an outstanding woman and Francois lied about the whole thing."

Maggie stared at her, tears welling up. "And I'll never get to the truth," she whispered.

"Bollocks!" Ellie took their dishes to the sink. "Notary Bouchard is an excellent judge of character, and he nailed both your grandmother's and Francois's characters on the head. We may never know what happened between your grandmother and your mother, but it doesn't change the fact that she kept you in her life, however she could."

"Grandmother never told my mom about Graham, or anything else. And Mom got so furious at not having a chance to search for him that she left home and never spoke to her again. So, yeah, I think we do know what happened."

Ellie ran the water in the sink and rattled the dishes around as she washed them. "That *is* a pretty shitty thing to do!"

Maggie pulled a letter out of her pocket and handed it to Ellie. "Here. This might explain things."

Ellie quickly dried her hands then read through the letter. "Well, okay, that puts things in a new light."

"It does. And I'm sorry, Ellie, I'm exhausted. The last few days have been overwhelming."

"Not everyone gets to win the Percyville Bake Fair," Ellie joked, trying to lighten both of their moods.

"No, they don't." Maggie grabbed a dish towel and dried as Ellie finished washing. "And we never did a thorough search of the cabin. It's obvious that place holds some serious memories for Octavie."

"Well, she kept the scrapbook there." Ellie put the last plate in the rack and wiped her hands. "We should take another look in the morning."

"After we visit the bakery." Maggie shelved a cup and leaned against the counter. "Let's give Veronique and Samuel a good start to their day. Then we'll come back and clean up."

"Have you thought more about what you're going to do with all this?"

"I can't let this place go." Maggie turned slowly, as if soaking up every atom of the room. "It just feels..."

"Like home?"

Maggie put her arm around Ellie and pulled her close. "Exactly! Like a part of me I never knew was missing."

They headed for the stairs, and Ellie gave the roll-top desk a shove to put it back in place against the wall. A loud thud stopped them in their tracks. Ellie knelt down to see what had fallen, then stood up with a book in her hand and handed it to Maggie.

Maggie blew the dust off the cover and opened it carefully. She read the first entry and her jaw dropped.

"It's my grandmother's diary!"

Chapter Twenty-Three

Maggie sat on the stairs with a thud, but Ellie pulled her up abruptly. "No, you don't. Get upstairs, put on your pajamas, brush your teeth, and *then* we'll settle in and read whatever your grandmother has to say."

Maggie ran up the stairs ahead of Ellie and they both got ready for bed in record time. They bumped into each other in the bathroom grabbing their toothbrushes and ran back to the room madly jumping on one of the beds.

"Here, we'll need this." Ellie grabbed the duvet and tucked it around their laps, pulling pillows from the head of the bed and placing them behind them so they could sit comfortably against the wall.

But Maggie sat still. The diary lay on her lap, and she hesitated before picking it up. "What if it's horrible?"

"But what if it explains everything?" Ellie nudged her. "Come on! I can't wait to hear it."

Maggie opened the cover to find that only a handful of pages had been used. But the writing was precise and delicate. Maggie took a deep breath and began to read.

January 1, 1945 – I'm not much of a writer and I don't know why Louise gave me this diary for Christmas, but maybe I'll write now and then. Especially now that the farm belongs to me. I still can't believe it. Aunt Marie surprised everyone and left it all to me! My parents refuse to speak to me. They think I am a fallen woman for living on my own. They want me to marry and have children, like a good woman should. Their dreams are not mine. I wasn't sure what I would do when I got back from secretary school in Montreal, but I want more than just being someone's wife. I will have to start looking for a job in the next few weeks. This winter is hard but there is plenty of wood – I chopped it myself for Aunt Marie in the fall, and fortunately the pantry is full. I will be fine. I went to the cabin to make sure all was well, and it is secure. The roof is solid and there are no leaks. It is quiet without Aunt Marie's laughter. She told the worst jokes, but they always made me smile. And I'm writing this all in English because Aunt Marie believed that having two languages made you stronger. "The world is full of interesting people and places," she used to say. "But make sure you can communicate with as many of them as you can." She was very smart. I took a lot of English classes while at school and I think I am quite good. I'm sure one day I will laugh at my mistakes, but I will try. And also, no one else here will be able to read my thoughts and feelings because very few can read English! I must go, I want to close some of the rooms upstairs for the next few months, just keep my bedroom open.

"Oh, Mags," Ellie whispered, "her own family didn't support her."

"Can you imagine?" Maggie shook her head, realizing what her grandmother had faced in those early years.

"Go on," Ellie said.

January 5, 1945 – Father Lapierre came to my door this morning and he had such a surprising project for me. He said it could be considered as me doing God's work. I don't visit his church much, but he visits me. He wants to use the farm as a way station for returning wounded soldiers. I asked why they were not just sent home or to hospitals. He was told they needed to be evaluated in a place they were familiar with, closer to home. Or at least that's what the doctor in charge believes. His name is Dr. Laurent and it's really his project, to see if this way of reintegrating soldiers is more helpful than just sending them home. They will rest here while the doctor evaluates them to see where they will go. Some will go home, others to hospitals for further therapy and care. He believes the environment of the farm will be beneficial to the men's mental health. No one talks about that, do they? People just treat the outward wounds. I hope this helps. I said yes.

January 6, 1945 – Dr. Laurent came to talk about what needs to be done, and I confess I am overwhelmed. He made a list of the things we will need and told me that he had hired some people from the village to help. A Dr. Fournier and his nurse assistant, Mme Savard, will come here the day before the first soldiers arrive. I have three bedrooms that will house three soldiers each. Cots will be brought, bedding, everything I need will be provided to me. The upstairs bathroom will be for the men, and the women will use the toilet on the main floor and the shower in the barn. No men will be allowed in the barn. The soldiers will use the living room and dining room and will only be able to walk around the garden. At least those who can. I asked for locks on my bedroom door and the barn. What have I let myself in for?

"She was very brave," Ellie said, trying not to read ahead over Maggie's shoulder.

January 8, 1945 – I met my helpers yesterday. A lovely young nurse, Emilie, will stay with me in my room, as she cannot go home every night. Madame Caron and her daughter Celine will do the cooking, cleaning and laundry. They live in the village and are very grateful for the pay. Everyone is. Celine's husband is at war and she has three small children. Philippe Aubin will help with the men, lifting those who need help and assisting them to bathe. He is very strong. He works in the stables but they have given him time off for this. We had a meeting yesterday morning and I wanted everyone to have a say in what happens here. They are to come to me with any complaints or problems and I will speak with Dr. Laurent as he is coordinating everything. We spent today bringing in the supplies. Philippe carried the cots up and we had them assembled and made up within hours. Extra bedding was provided and a truck arrived early this morning with enough food to feed an army, or at least our small group. The food will be replenished as needed. Madame Caron was delighted and set about rearranging my kitchen to make room for everything. She has my blessing. We all dined together and were quite pleased with what we had accomplished. I'm told the soldiers will be arriving in two days. Tomorrow morning we will meet Dr. Fournier and his assistant, Mme Savard. I must sleep.

January 9, 1945 – Dr. Fournier is a rough man and Mme Savard has no heart. I will not tolerate tyrants nor will I be ordered about in my own home. I understand rules and they must be followed for the sake of the soldiers and their health, but not at the expense of these good people who help me run the farm for their benefit. My blood is boiling. Tomorrow the first soldiers will arrive and we will welcome them. Thank goodness Dr. Fournier and his dragon will only be here for a few hours each day. Emilie will take care of emergencies and if anything serious happens, Dr. Fournier will be called.

January 25, 1945 – So much has happened. So many young men wounded. My heart breaks every time a new soldier comes through the door. They are scared, exhausted, and just want to go home. Most of them do. Some need further care and are sent on to hospitals. But most of these men are from this area. I know a few by name, most by face, some through a friend of a friend. They are so happy to see us that I have to be brave and not cry in front of them. Especially those with terrible wounds. I am so tired. I will try to write more later.

February 15, 1945 – Our rooms have been full and empty, depending on the fighting overseas, or so I am told. We had a couple of days last week to collect ourselves, do a major cleaning of all the rooms and laundry, and gather as a group, minus Col. Dr. Fournier (that's what we call him!). Everyone needed a good night's sleep and we finally had two days. Tomorrow, we receive five more soldiers. But I want to write about something that happened last week. It took us all by surprise. A young man, Pierre Lebrun, arrived without knowing who he was, and he had nightmares that kept everyone awake. He was screaming and thrashing about. I decided to put him in the barn, and Emilie stayed with him. She told us in the morning that she had slept, mainly because Pierre had slept. He had gone to the cow, put his head on her shoulder, stroked her and whispered words that Emilie could not hear. Then he went to sleep and didn't dream. Could it have been the sounds of the animals around him that comforted him? His family arrived the next day, and, poor soul, he did not recognize them. He was polite and agreed to leave with them, believing them when they told him he was their son. His family was just thrilled that he'd come home to them. Dr. Fournier was very abrupt, telling them that he might never remember his past or them. Pierre's father kept a straight face, but his mother broke down. Pierre went to her and hugged her, even though she was a stranger to him. But the most amazing thing happened after Dr. Fournier left the room. Mme Savard came to the family, took their hands, including Pierre's, and said that Pierre could very well regain his memories. Sometimes all it took was time. In front of Pierre, she told his parents to treat him as they always had, to tease and joke with him, take him to places he's familiar with. Where there is love, there is always hope. And then she rushed off after the doctor, leaving everyone in the room stunned. But the family was hopeful. The "dragon woman" has a heart after all.

March 12, 1945 – Emilie has been having problems with Mme Savard. They are like oil and water. Nothing Emilie does is good enough for that woman! When Mme Savard scolds her, Emilie remains quiet and takes it. I stood up for her a few times when Mme Savard was wrong, and she did not like that. But away from the older nurse, Emilie is a joy to work with. The soldiers love her, and I believe she has had two offers of marriage, which she declined.

March 30, 1945 – Mme Savard has been away for a few days, and we have just been told by Dr. Fournier that she has lost her son in the war. We had made up all sorts of stories among ourselves, and some of them not too kind, but Dr. Fournier could have told us sooner. She will be back tomorrow. I feel sorry for the things I thought about her. She is a mother who has lost a son, and none of us knew she even had a son. I hope she is well.

April 2, 1945 – Mme Savard returned, still in command of her nursing skills and take-charge attitude, but with a slump in her shoulders. We offered her our condolences, and although her eyes were bright with tears, she never cried in front of us. Emilie told me that night she found Mme Savard behind the barn, weeping uncontrollably. Emilie took her into the barn and told her to speak to the cow, explaining how it had helped a soldier. And she did. She leaned against the warmth of the animal and whispered in her ear for almost ten minutes. Emilie was worried the older woman had become ill, but Mme Savard stepped away from the cow, gave Emilie a quick hug, and marched out of the barn. We are all human.

"Poor woman," Maggie said, taking a minute to catch her breath from her nonstop reading.

April 14, 1945 – I am so tired. Some of the men are so nice, very polite and grateful for everything we do. Others are not. We cannot begin to understand what they have been through or what they are still experiencing, and we make exceptions and go about our day. But I am so tired. I fell into bed last night and cried. I thought I was quiet, but I felt Emilie climb into bed next to me and wrap her arms around me. I felt her body tremble with her own exhaustion. I woke up today to find my clothes laid out and the water bowl filled with hot water. Emilie was already up and she let me sleep a little longer. I wish she was my sister!

"Sounds like you and me," Ellie leaned into Maggie's shoulder and gave her a gentle nudge. Maggie returned the gesture and continued reading.

April 25, 1945 – Jean Fabien's mother came to pick him up today. He is a wonderful young man. He lost his right hand. He seemed to be doing well, but he opened up to me on the day he had the room to himself. He shared that he was studying to be an architect, but will not be able to continue now that he cannot write. He had to stay longer than most because Dr. Fournier wanted to treat his infection here. He only has his mother at home, and they didn't think she could take care of him properly. But while he was here, I helped him learn to write with his other hand. He was so determined. The others helped him too, whether it was giving him ideas or just encouragement, and when he was ready to be released, he wrote a letter to his mother asking her to come and get him. I don't know if he will be able to continue his studies, but I told him to let me know.

May 1, 1945 – Mme Savard has been coming back in the evenings to read to the soldiers. She brought her late son's favorite book and has raided my meager bookshelf to entertain the soldiers. They love her. She has also become less combative with Emilie, and Emilie in turn makes sure that Mme Savard has a cup of tea and some of my cookies in the evening when she comes. When Mme Savard started sharing her cookies with the young men, we made sure that her plate was always full. A sad thing happened today. Denis Lambert arrived yesterday. Although his eyes are open, he doesn't respond to any kind of stimulation and has been in Philippe's care since he arrived. Dr. Fournier fears that he will have to be institutionalized. Unfortunately, we all know what that means.

May 27, 1945 – We've put in the garden, and the men who can walk on their own often come and sit outside while we work. A couple have been allowed to help, and although they are slow, the activity helps them immensely. Louis Trudel joined us yesterday. He lost a leg and is very upset. He loves to dance, as does his fiancée, but he's afraid she'll leave him because of his injury. I told him, rather abruptly, that if she thought he was less of a man because of his loss, she wasn't worth his worry. Mme Savard overheard our conversation and told him that he could be fitted for an artificial leg when he left, and with practice and patience, he would be able to dance again. His eyes lit up with excitement and Mme Savard left with a smile on her face. She has become more than just a nurse making rounds with the doctor.

June 7, 1945 – An interesting thing happened today. A young soldier, Dominique Michaud, arrived with his own doctor! A big bear of a man with red hair and a neat beard, blue eyes and a lovely accent. His name is Graham. I met him at the cabin today. I was taking a short break when Graham walked up the path. I told him as sternly as I could that the soldiers should stay at the farm. Graham told me that he wasn't injured and explained his situation. He then marveled at the man who had opened his farm for the wounded. I brushed past him and said "That man is me!" I was so proud of what we have accomplished here. Emilie teased me before bed and said I was smiling a lot.

"Oh, ho!" Ellie clapped her hands in delight. "Your grandmother was a spitfire."

"And this is such a cute meet," Maggie grinned. "So, this is my grandfather?"

"Seems to be, but read on. I can't wait to find out what happens."

Chapter Twenty-Four

"Come on," Ellie said impatiently. "Please continue!"

June 9, 1945 – Dominique has left. His father collected him this morning and Mr. Michaud suggested that Graham stay here for the duration of the war to help out. Dr. Fournier said that was not possible (I don't know why). I don't know when Graham has to leave but I hope it's not too soon. He has been a big help. He's been sleeping in the soldier's rooms but if we need the bed, he'll have to sleep in the barn.

June 12, 1945 – This man is everywhere! If I'm working at the laundry, he makes sure my basket is not too heavy. If I'm carrying food to the soldiers, he takes the trays from my hands and goes upstairs. When I'm sitting in the garden at the end of the day, he's nearby, sharing stories with the soldiers, or helping some of them improve their English. He speaks French very well and has complimented me on my English when I speak with him. His eyes crinkle when he smiles.

"This is even better than a romance novel!" Ellie said.

"Since when do you read romance novels?" Maggie asked.

"Well, I..." Ellie leaned over and peered at the pages. "I think we should keep reading. It's getting late."

"There's no way I'm going to bed without finishing this."

June 15, 1945 – We had a terrible storm pass through. The power went out for a day, but Graham got the outdoor stove going and we managed to get everyone a hot meal. The water for cleaning was boiled on the campfire and he made sure to carry it to the kitchen. Emilie tried once and got a bad burn. Dr. Fournier was not there, but Graham took care of it. Emilie was practically giddy over him.

June 18, 1945 – He brought me flowers, from my own garden!

Ellie snorted with delight.

"Hey," Maggie defended him, "at least he tried to woo her."

"Woo her?" Ellie swallowed what she was about to say when she saw how involved Maggie was in her grandparents' courtship. "You're right. It was really romantic for the time."

June 20, 1945 – Celine has been bringing her children with her for the last few days. Adeline, their babysitter, is ill. She sets the two eldest to work, gathering small sticks for the fire, or practicing their reading with the soldiers in the garden. They are good children. But Thomas, the oldest, ran down to the creek when no one was looking. No one heard the little scream except Graham (of course), and he was able to run down and pull Thomas out, soaking wet and scared. He said he was fishing, but when Graham asked him where his rod was, he admitted that he had just been jumping rocks and fell in. Graham said he would get them both some rods the next day and they would catch fish for dinner. And they did! They came back with five large brook trout. Thomas carried the one he caught, and Graham told everyone that the young boy had actually caught it all by himself. I think Graham is too perfect. There must be a flaw.

"At least she's not overwhelmed by him," Maggie muttered.

Ellie bit her tongue, not wanting to give away her deep love of romance. She'd never hear the end of it.

June 23, 1945 – He came to the cabin this evening and sat on the porch with me. We hardly spoke, but watched the stars come out. He wanted to make sure I was okay. I needed his comfort more than I knew. One of the soldiers, Gaston Labelle, hanged himself in the barn last night, and I found him this morning when I went for my shower. I ran for Graham, and he came immediately, and cut the poor boy down and covered him with a blanket before anyone else could see. When Dr. Fournier arrived, I told him what had happened, and he was visibly shocked. I've never seen him show any emotion, but the plight of this soldier touched him. The family arrived at noon and took their son home for burial. It was a very quiet day. News travels fast.

"Can you imagine what she saw in those months?" Maggie pulled the duvet higher up her chest, as if a cool breeze had swept through the room.

"She's a tough cookie." Ellie helped her pull the duvet and made sure they were both cocooned and warm.

June 28, 1945 – He Kissed Me! Just before lunch, as I was carrying in a basket of tomatoes for Mme Caron, he reached out a hand and pulled me to him and gave me a quick kiss. He grinned and said that life was too short to wonder, and then he went on to the back of the house where I heard the sound of an axe in the woods and someone whistling a happy tune. Did anyone see us? I can't believe this is happening!

July 3, 1945 – Graham told me that he has to leave in a few days. He got a letter, and he has no choice. They are sending him back to fight. I am full of emotions. Fear for him, heartbroken that he is leaving, and something that sits in the pit of my stomach. Dread. He is leaving.

"Oh, no!" Ellie said.

"Wait, wait, let's see what happened."

July 4, 1945 – He came to the cabin tonight and he told me he loved me. He gathered me close and we stood together for a long time, our hearts beating together. How silly is that? But that's how it felt. And then he kissed me again and we ended up together. I can't even write this. I should feel shame and guilt, but I do not. I love him too. Can this be real? Can you fall in love so quickly?

"And there it is," Maggie said. "Proof that Graham is my grandfather."

"Well, not exactly, but..."

"Oh, come on!"

"Keep reading."

July 5, 1945 – Graham is leaving tomorrow. He wants to go to Father Lapierre and ask him to marry us right away! I said no. I want him to come home and we will have a proper ceremony, nothing rushed or hurried. A little part of me wants to be sure that he loves me, as much as I love him. He agreed, but asked me to wait for him. I said of course I would. He apologized for not having a ring, but I said I didn't need one. All I wanted was for him to come back to me. Everyone knows what is going on between us. And Mme Savard arranged for Graham and I to spend one last full night together in the cabin. She brought us some food and said good night. We didn't get much sleep.

"Okay, that's more like it," Ellie said.

"Look at this," Maggie pointed to the next entry. The words were legible but smudged. "Tears?"

"Looks like it."

July 6, 1945 – He is gone. And he took my heart. I don't care how silly that sounds, but I gave it fully. I have an address where I can write to him and he said he would live for my letters. And I his, though he didn't know where he was going or how soon our letters would cross. I held on to him until Mme Savard gently took my arm. It was more for Graham's sake I realized later, when Emilie told me he could hardly keep from crying. So now we wait and return to the business at hand. The soldiers have come and gone. The week ahead looks quiet and we have a lot of cleaning to do. I will work and keep myself busy.

July 15, 1945 – Louise has returned from school in Montreal to stay. Her mother died last month and the house by the church is now hers. She comes over every day and helps in any way she can. I've told her about Graham and she almost fainted. Mme Savard took her aside one day and when they thought I hadn't noticed, they put their heads together and had quite the chat. They both think I'm worrying too much about Graham. But I don't even talk about him. And I'm not very hungry these days. It must be the heat.

July 30, 1945 – I've written so many letters to him, and never heard back. Until today! I grabbed the letter from the startled postman and ran to the cabin where I slowly opened it. My stomach has been acting up and the stress of not hearing from him made me sleep terribly. But he loves me. He says he can't wait to see me again and to remember that I promised to wait. How can I not? He sent an old, scratched ring in the envelope. He apologized again that it was not more, but I put it on my finger immediately and will never take it off. Louise is very happy for me, but she wants me to eat more.

August, 15, 1945 – We had so many soldiers last week that we had to put cots in the barn for a few days. Now that Louise is back, she demanded that Emilie and I use her house to shower. She didn't think it was right for us to use the barn shower. I have to admit that she has a nice bathroom. Her mother had it redone just before she died. There is a perfect claw foot tub and plenty of hot water! The few moments alone I find while soaking is heaven. My, how shallow I've become.

August 17, 1945 – I have not heard from Graham since his one and only letter. The soldiers assure me that's normal, especially if he's moving around. Every time new soldiers arrive, a soldier who has been here for a while tells them about the great "romance". Sometimes it's embarrassing. But it gives them something to think about besides their own problems. Most are in good shape, if not physically, then outwardly so. But we all know how deceptive a smile can be during the day, only to hear a cry in the night.

August 24, 1945 – I am sure. I am pregnant.

"I knew it!" Maggie said.

"Looks like your mother had an interesting beginning," Ellie said.

Chapter Twenty-Five

September 1, 1945 – I finally told Louise because I was trying so hard to keep my food down, and Mme Caron kept making comments on how pale I was. I kept blaming the heat, as it has been very hot this summer, but she had seven children of her own before her husband died and she knows the signs. Mme Savard is also suspicious, but has been very kind. She makes sure I am well hydrated and gives me bland biscuits first thing in the morning. She has taken to spending a great deal of the day here and her help is much appreciated. Dr. Fournier was not too pleased when he found out, but she threatened to stop working with him altogether. She is a good dragon to have on your side!

September 4, 1945 – THE WAR IS OVER! We had such a celebration when we heard the news! The soldiers are being diverted from our farm and only a few remain. I ran to the cabin last night and cried for hours with relief. Graham is coming home! I fell asleep there and woke up to find a hot bowl of porridge on the table. I slept until Louise came in, but I ate the whole bowl. It was delicious! There is so much to do to get the remaining soldiers ready to leave. It's already quieter.

Maggie stifled a yawn.

"Do you want to continue this tomorrow?"

Maggie flipped through the remaining pages. "Not a chance. I need to see how this story ends."

"Oh, thank goodness," Ellie slipped down on the pillows, pulled the blanket over her shoulders and settled in like a child listening to her favorite story.

September 5, 1945 – The last soldiers leaves tomorrow morning. I've asked everyone who helped to come and see him off. Louise is knitting baby clothes. I can't wait to tell Graham. I know he will be pleased. I have to speak to Father Lapierre, but I'm afraid of what he will say.

September 6, 1945 – They are all gone. The soldiers left before noon and we all made a feast for lunch. We pulled the chairs and tables outside under the cool of the trees and we sat around talking for hours, sharing stories of what we'd been through the past months. They were all well paid for their work and excited to move on with their lives, some more so than others. Emilie is going to Montreal to continue her education, and hopes to find a good job at the hospital. Mme Savard has assured her that she will write a glowing reference for her. Celine received a telegram that her husband will be returning soon. Philippe is going to open his own furniture making shop with his father as his helper. He is tired of horses! Mme Caron is looking forward to a rest. Dr. Fournier left quickly after signing off the last soldier's papers, but Mme Savard stayed. She doesn't know what she will do but she doesn't want to continue working for Dr. Fournier. She thought about finding a hospital where soldiers with more serious injuries were placed. She enjoyed helping them. Before they left, everyone helped strip the beds and dismantle the cots. Philippe, Emilie and Louise took everything to the barn to be picked up by the army next week. Mme Caron said she would be back tomorrow to wash the linens, but I told her it could wait a few days. Louise went home as well, but returned for supper with an onion soup and crusty bread for what she called a comfort meal. We sat on the porch and watched the stars and listened to the frogs in the creek. The silence was both disturbing and comforting at the same time. I can't explain it. I've been busy since January and now I can sit and do nothing and not feel guilty. Louise offered to stay with me, since it would be the first time in months that I would be alone, but I told her to come back tomorrow. I need to be alone. I have not heard from Graham.

October 9, 1945 – I went to a doctor who didn't know me, and he said I was healthy and everything seemed to be fine. I pretended to be married, wearing Graham's ring on my wedding finger. Still no letters.

October 30, 1945 – Louise is such a nuisance. She is here every day and watches me like a hawk. But she is my best friend, and she knows how I feel. She's not a nuisance. She is my rock. We had a long talk last night. I am sure that Graham has changed his mind about me. She says to give it time. Anything could have happened. I agreed. He could be dead. She got very upset at that. I feel very naïve to believe that he wanted anything more than a little fun. But I've made my bed, as my mother would say. And I will live in it. The baby is due in the spring and I have much to do before then. My money will not last long, and with another mouth to feed I will have to come up with something to get us through.

November 15, 1945 – I think I have found something that will help. I baked a birthday cake for Celine's son. Chocolate with sparkles. Aunt Marie had some in a jar in the back cupboard! I never thought of her as a sparkle kind of person. Celine paid me for it with a bushel of apples from her crop. Mrs. Drouin heard about the cake and asked me to make one with sparkles for her husband's birthday. She paid me in money! I made two more for neighbors, and Monsieur Gratton at the village store asked me if I could make smaller things, like croissants and such. I told him yes, and he has ordered a dozen for the weekend.

December 1, 1945 – What a day! Monsieur Gratton has asked for more baked goods for his shop, and I can hardly keep up! I put the money I make straight into the shoebox in my room for safekeeping. I find that having the oven on all day while I bake keeps the place very warm indeed. Oh, the baby just moved!

January 22, 1946 – I should write more, but I don't have the time. Christmas came so fast, and I created original cakes for various friends as presents. And now I have paid orders to make them! I've tried other pastries and Louise has been a willing tester. I swear she has gained weight! I took a chance and went home to see my parents for the holidays, to go to church with them. They took one look at me and refused to let me in the house. I should have known what to expect, but I tried. I will be all right.

February 3, 1946 – I met Mme Yvette in Mr. Gratton's store today. She is a witch. She made a comment about where my husband was, glancing directly at my belly

(I am big). I have had to accept that Graham has either forgotten about me or died. For some reason I can accept the latter, and told Mme Yvette that my husband died during the war. She didn't believe me, nor did some of the others who witnessed her behavior, but others called her out and told her to leave me alone. I held my head up and finished my shopping. Louise asked me why I didn't write to Graham and tell him about the baby. I don't want to be one of those women who uses a baby to get a man. As much as I feel good about the baby, when I meet people like Mme Yvette, my courage falters. And Graham knows where I am.

February 18, 1946 – Paulette Legault came to my door this morning in a terrible blizzard. The wind was so bad that she had to hold on to the railings to keep from being blown off the porch. I pulled her inside and as soon as I had helped her out of her coat and brought her into the kitchen near the stove to warm up, I saw that she was in trouble. A terrible bruise covered one side of her face, and her eye was swollen shut. She was shivering, and not just from the cold. I wrapped a blanket around her, made her a hot cup of tea and gave her a piece of apple pie. We sat in silence. Her hands clutched that cup of tea like a lifeline. Her story came out slowly, as if she were afraid to say the words aloud. She had just married and moved here, and her family still lived near Quebec City. She was so far from home. Her husband was not a nice man. I knew about him. She said she would not go back to him, but she wanted to go home. She had run away from him that morning with only the clothes on her back. She stayed with me for two days during the storm and we made a plan. When Louise arrived on the third day, we asked her for help. I took money from my shoebox and arranged for Louise to drive her to the train station that night and get her a ticket home to Quebec City. From there, she assured me, she could reach her family. I never want to be under someone's thumb like that. Ever.

March 30, 1946 – The baby moves all the time! I am having trouble filling my orders, but Louise has become my assistant for some things. She is more excited about the baby than I am. The good news is that the snow is melting early this year! And Mme Legault has made it to her family. They want her to go back to her husband, but she has vowed to be like me and live on her own. She has secured a in Montreal and will live with an elderly aunt. That sounds so familiar!

April, 1946 – My darling baby girl, Florence, was born in the dark hours of the night on the 15th. I named her after Graham's mother because ... well, I thought it was right. She has red hair and strong lungs. Louise is staying here for a while to help me. I am so tired.

May, 1946 – Louise says I need to see the doctor because I cry too much. I didn't want to talk to a male doctor, so I contacted Mme Savard. She said that what I'm feeling is very common and I shouldn't worry unless there were no good points in my days. Which there are. She said I shouldn't try to suppress my feelings and just let them flow through me. I did that yesterday in front of Louise, I cried like a baby for a few minutes, then wiped my face, picked up Florence, put her in my backpack and went for a walk. I felt much better when I got back. And the baking helps. I can hardly keep up, but the security of the money helps to ease my worries.

July 30, 1946 – The garden is planted and Florence is growing by leaps and bounds. She loves to be outside with me and the barn cat has become her protector, sitting at her feet whenever Florence is outside. I've made a big decision – I'm starting my own business. My good friend, Jean-Philippe, came by last week. He finished school and is a notary! How fancy. But he was always smart. I will have to address him as Maitre Bouchard from now on! I asked him what it takes to start a business, and we sat for two hours going over what will be needed. It's a lot, but he assured me that he would take care of the legal aspect. When I asked him what his fees would be, he brushed it off and refused to take any money. But I will have to make sure he gets some of my baked goods in the future. I've also decided to stop dreaming about Graham. Oh, yes, I still do. Louise once asked me why I don't look for him. I'm too afraid and ashamed. Afraid to find him dead. Ashamed to find him and tell him I had a daughter – he would think I was trying to trap him. Yes, I know, he wanted to marry me before he left. But he has not been in touch all this time, and he knows where I am. Maybe my pride is too much and I should try. But I'm so tired. I will keep my love for him alive in Florence. What will I tell her about her father? That he died in the war. That's all I can do. And this will be my last entry for a while. The business will take up all my time and Florence will be crawling before I know it. Mme Savard came to visit and took one look at her and knew the truth. She smiled, hugged me, and played on the floor with her for an hour. Life is full of the unknown. I am excited. We will be okay.

"Is that it?" Ellie asked.

Maggie flipped through the rest of the diary but every page was blank. "Yes."

They sat quietly, digesting what they had learned.

Ellie threw back the blanket, stood up and stretched before moving to her own bed and snuggling in under the covers. "Well, I think we know that your grandmother was a pretty amazing woman."

Maggie adjusted the duvet and pillows, and placed the diary on the nightstand beside her. She turned off the light and lay still for a few minutes.

"She was," she said at last. "And now I'm sure she would approve of what I'm doing for Veronique and Samuel."

She turned to look at Ellie, only to find her friend lying there with her eyes closed, her soft rhythmic breathing filling the room.

Chapter Twenty-Six

Breakfast consisted of the remaining eggs and toast with the last sliced tomato on their plates. They ate and had everything cleaned up and put away in record time. They were both tired from their late night of reading, but looking forward to the day ahead.

"I think this will be enough." Maggie looked around the living room at the work they had done the night before. They had straightened the furniture and tossed anything that couldn't be repaired into the garbage.

Ellie slipped on her shoes and grabbed her purse. "Walk or drive?"

Maggie checked the sky and tied her running shoes. "Walk. I need to figure out what to say."

They locked the front door, knowing that all sets of keys were now accounted for, and walked down the driveway with a sense of purpose.

As they neared the church, they saw Mrs. Ethier sitting on her porch. She waved, and they walked through the graveyard toward her. Ellie's head swung back and forth as she tried to read the old tombstones as they passed.

"Thank you for calling the police," Maggie said as she stopped at the bottom of the porch. Mrs. Ethier rocked slowly in her chair, as if each push with the toe of her shoe took all her energy. "But I'm sorry about Francois."

"You shouldn't be," she said. "He was not a good man."

"We were thankful the officer returned all the stolen goods though," Ellie said.

"Octavie would have been appalled." The older woman shivered as if the ghost of her old friend had put a hand on her shoulder. "Your grandmother had a way with words that kept Francois in his place *most* of the time, but he was wild."

"We found Grandmother's diary last night."

Mrs. Ethier's eyes widened and she grinned. "I never knew she used it!"

"And we know all about how the farm was used, Mme Savard, Graham coming here, and what Octavie went through when Florence was born," Ellie said with a huge grin, as if reliving every entry they had read the night before.

"And I want to thank you for being such a good friend to my grandmother," Maggie said. She ran up the stairs and gave the woman a big hug.

Mrs. Ethier held her close. "She was like a sister to me."

"And I'm going to sell the bakery to Veronique and Samuel," Maggie blurted out.

Mrs. Ethier pulled away and let her go. "Why?"

The question surprised Maggie. "Well, because my grandmother had a great deal of respect for them, and they love the business. I know what it's like to start out."

"But they're not starting out," Mrs. Ethier reminded her. "They're getting a whole lucrative brand, and everything that goes with it."

"Don't you like them?" Ellie asked. "Is there something you want to tell Maggie about them?"

"No, no." The older woman waved her hand as if to brush aside her own words. "I couldn't bear to see you lose what your grandmother worked so hard for."

"But I won't." Maggie smiled at her. "I'll keep a good portion of the shares in the company, but I have my own business, and I'd like to make a name for myself, on my own." She nodded back towards the farmhouse. "I now have an amazing farm and cute little cabin. I'm not a greedy person. What I have makes me happy."

Mrs. Ethier studied her for a moment. "I was wrong. Octavie would be proud of what you're doing. I don't meet many people like you anymore."

"Like what?" Maggie asked.

"Kind and thoughtful."

"You don't mean..."

"I've lived a long time, Marguerite." Mrs. Ethier sighed. "I've seen a lot and dealt with all sorts of people. I am not an optimist these days."

"Well, would it be all right if I stopped by when I come back for a visit?" Maggie asked her. "I'm going to be back and forth a lot, and my grandmother's house feels like..."

"Home?" The old woman raised an inquiring eyebrow.

"Exactly!" Maggie stole a glance at Ellie. "I've got a lot of things to go through, maybe a few mysteries to solve while I'm at it."

"You'd be most welcome, my dear," she said as she headed for her front door. "Go tell Veronique and Samuel the good news. The town will be buzzing by nightfall."

***

They continued down the main street, stopping now and then to peer into store windows. They could see the Tavie Bakery sign from almost any angle on the street. Not garish or intrusive, but quaint and inviting, and within a few minutes, they were once again standing outside the front door.

Maggie hesitated.

"What's wrong?" Ellie bumped into her friend and braced herself against the doorframe.

"I'm scared." Maggie turned to Ellie. "Am I doing the right thing?"

"What does your gut say?"

"It's been wrong before."

"Rarely," Ellie huffed in disbelief.

Maggie didn't answer, instead she pushed open the door and took a deep whiff of the various pastries fresh from the oven. Veronique was serving a few customers, and she gave Maggie and Ellie a quick wave, then a raised a finger to tell them she'd be right with them.

The customers knew who Maggie was, and even though they'd made their purchases, they didn't leave. Instead, they meandered around, pretending to inspect other delicacies in the display cases.

Veronique beckoned Maggie and Ellie to join her in the back room. Samuel walked over from the storeroom with a large sack of flour. He set it on the floor near the workstation and wiped his hands on his apron. "Good to see you again so soon, Maggie."

"Yes, well," Maggie shifted from one foot to the other. "I've made a decision about the bakery." She caught them stealing glances at each other and noticed Veronique's white-knuckled grip before she hid her fists behind her back.

The shop fell silent as the low chatter of customers in the front ceased. The only sound was the deep whirring of the large oven in the corner.

"I have a proposition for you." Maggie stole a quick, reassuring glance at Ellie, who smiled and nodded for her to continue. "I'd like to sell you a majority stake in Tavie Bakery, which will include the bakery, the brand, and the recipes, to be paid over time at a reasonable rate."

"Oh, mon dieu!" Veronique staggered, and Samuel caught her and held her tight.

"You're selling us everything?" he asked.

"No," Maggie shook her head. "I still want a share, but you'll be the majority shareholders. This was my grandmother's, and I can't let go of everything she created. I need to have a piece of her."

"Of course, of course!" Veronique pulled Maggie into a rib-crunching hug, tears streaming down her face. She stepped back and wiped them away. "I'm so sorry. We thought..."

When Samuel realized his wife couldn't continue, he jumped in. "We thought you were going to ask us to leave and take it over yourself. We did some research on you and your Cozy Corner Café. You're making quite a name for yourself."

"Thank you." Maggie smiled. "It's been a lot of work, and I understand what running a business like this means. Octavie thought very highly of both of you, and I want to... pass on some good fortune."

"Oh, this is such wonderful news, Veronique." They all turned to see the two older women who had just bought a dozen pastries between them. They were as excited as the young couple who would become the new owners of Tavie Bakery.

Maggie tried to speak over the congratulations and Veronique's squeals of joy. "My notary, Notary Bouchard, will be in touch with you soon with the paperwork. But I wanted to come and tell you the news myself."

Then it was Samuel's turn to hug her, and he went on to hug Ellie, then the two women customers. "How are we going to get through the day?"

"The same as any other," Veronique told him. "With smiles and delicious pastries!"

Chapter Twenty-Seven

They strolled back to the farmhouse, and Maggie swung her arms as if the weight of the world had been lifted from her shoulders. She smiled and nodded at people who greeted her, marveling at how comfortable she felt in this small town. Maybe it was a genetic thing.

They passed the church and Ellie veered off towards the cemetery. "You promised!" she called over her shoulder, turning to make sure Maggie was following her into the cool of the woods that led to the cemetery.

"I did indeed," Maggie said as she followed Ellie along the lanes of tombstones, stopping beside her as Ellie took pictures of the inscriptions or ran her hand over the rough surface, tracing the names and dates with her fingers.

"Look at this one," Ellie whispered, her tone hushed. She was always respectful when she walked among the dead. She framed and photographed an elegant marker with carved flowers and birds flowing along the sides.

Maggie looked closely and read the inscription. "Adrianne Duprat." She turned to Ellie, confused. "Relative?"

"Maybe." Ellie moved down the row and stopped again, pointing to a less ornate gravestone.

Maggie read the name and raised an eyebrow. "Joseph Duprat." She scanned the names of the other tombstones around them. "Could this be a family plot?"

"They're pretty old," Ellie noted. "A lot of them circa 1835." She paused, staring at the stones as if searching for the answer. "If I remember correctly, a cholera epidemic decimated the area around that time. Maybe the whole family caught it."

"Ellie." Maggie stopped in the middle of the path. When she got her friend's attention, she gestured to the surrounding graves. "Are all these people related to me? No one told me where the family came from. I only knew the last name, but this..." She couldn't finish the thought.

"You definitely have a family, Mags." Ellie smiled at her. "Maybe something to investigate?"

"That would be amazing!" Maggie grinned and walked around, discovering more Duprat names.

Ellie followed her, photographing every tombstone with the Duprat name, double checking her camera to make sure the pictures were clear, and retaking those that weren't. They covered the entire cemetery from top to bottom. "I wish I had my rubbing tools with me, but these photos will have to do for now."

"But who else belongs in this family tree?" Maggie asked, standing by the grave of Marcel Duprat.

"We'll find out when I get started," Ellie said, bending down to take another photo.

"You're really enjoying this, aren't you?"

"Oh, Maggie." Ellie grinned. "You have no idea how much I love this!"

"And we know where the cemetery is and we can come back anytime, right?"

"Indeed." Ellie glanced around. "I think we've covered all the Duprats and..." she looked at her watch, "... holy moly, it's already lunchtime!"

Maggie checked her own watch in stunned surprise. "We've been here for two hours."

"Time flies when you're having fun."

"I never imagined walking through a graveyard would be fun."

"Welcome to my world. Now let's go back. I'm starving!"

***

"I'm done here," Maggie said, her head buried deep in the refrigerator. She stepped back, a wet cloth in her hand, the shelves before her now empty. "Clean as a whistle. Next time I come, I'll bring exactly what I need."

"Or buy from the store in town," Ellie said. "And I hear the bakery here is quite spectacular."

Maggie rinsed her cloth and returned it to the hook under the counter. "I can't believe how high Veronique's squeal was."

Ellie nodded. "You did a good thing, Maggie. They were both so excited."

Maggie brushed it off with a shake of her head. "I'm sure it's what my grandmother would have wanted me to do. Now, I'll take a quick run upstairs, check that everything's in order and locked, and then we can go to the cabin."

While Maggie went upstairs, Ellie did the same on the main floor, checking the windows, aligning a chair under the table, plumping a cushion for its next occupant—who would be Maggie!

Thumping feet on the stairs announced Maggie's return. After putting their overnight bags in the car and locking the front door, Maggie took the box containing the items stolen from the cabin and they headed down the path and through the woods.

The water flowed under the wooden bridge with a quiet gurgle. Maggie ran her hand along the railing, wondering what this part of the property had looked like all those years ago when Graham and Octavie had made it their own.

She unlocked the cabin door, and they stepped inside. Though the room was small and intimate, it felt complete.

"Do you smell that?" Ellie asked her as she took a deep sniff. A hint arose over the mustiness of a closed building.

"I do." Maggie set the box down on the table and hesitated, her nose in the air, breathing deeply until the dust made her sneeze.

"Flowers," Ellie said. "But I can't tell what kind."

"How is it possible that the smell is still here?"

"And I'm sure your grandmother come here often," Ellie said. "Otherwise, there'd be a lot more dust."

Maggie returned the items from the box to their respective places in the room. "I don't know why I assumed she never came back after Graham left."

"I'd return to the scene of a great love," Ellie said.

"True." Maggie noticed a hint of melancholy in her friend. "But you live in the house of your great love."

Ellie smiled. "It doesn't hurt so much, Maggie. I still see Adam and Winnie around sometimes, not *them*, but things around me remind me of them."

"They'll always be with you."

"Always." Ellie held the scrapbook in her hands, kneading the cover. "What the?" She opened the cover and showed it to Maggie.

"What?"

"Look." Ellie grabbed Maggie's hand and ran it over the inside back cover. "There's something in here."

"What could it..." Maggie started, but Ellie had already pulled out her pocketknife and was gently sliding it under the edge of the lining. Maggie froze, wondering what her grandmother could have hidden.

"Let's see what we've got here." Ellie carefully peeled back the sheet and slid her finger into the gap. After a few seconds of wiggling, she pulled out a folded piece of paper. She handed it to Maggie, then held the opening to her eyes and peered inside. There was another piece of paper at the top corner. After more wiggling, the second paper landed in her hand.

Maggie held the first page as if it were something that might bite.

"Oh, for goodness sake, open it!" Ellie bounced on her feet, excited by the discovery.

With trembling fingers, Maggie unfolded the paper and held it open. She read it and looked at Ellie, her eyes wide with surprise.

"What does it say?" Ellie took it from Maggie. "Holy moly!"

The birth certificate she was holding wobbled as she reread it again. It showed the baptism of Florence Duprat, born May 17, 1945, mother Octavie Duprat, father Graham Brodie of Moose River, New Brunswick.

"Here, here." Ellie slipped the second piece of paper into Maggie's hands and waited.

Maggie opened it to reveal a faded handwritten letter. "Oh, no!" Maggie shoved it at Ellie. "This is too much. Please read it for me."

"Let's sit down." Ellie moved to the two chairs and gave them and the table a quick dust off with her hand before spreading the letter out full on the table. "*My Darling O.*" Ellie covered her mouth with her hand. "Oh, this is going to be a love letter!"

Maggie stared at her, a smile appearing. "Continue."

"*My Darling O, I returned to my unit with minimal damage. The details would bore you, but I am in one piece. I apologize for not answering your letters right away, but I could not. I miss you every day and cannot wait to get back to you. I am being sent "away" and...*"

"What does 'away' mean?" Maggie asked.

"It was war-time, he could have been forbidden to tell her where he was going in case his letter was confiscated."

"Smart. Okay."

"*Our unit is moving, but I will try to write. My time with you is what I will hold in my heart to get through the coming days. We hope for a quick end, but no one knows for sure. I stole a flower from your garden when I left, and I keep it in my wallet. The scent is fading, but I imagine I can smell the field by the wooden bridge and the vase of flowers you kept on the table in the cabin. I must go, but believe me when I say that you have my heart, now and always. Until we are together again, I remain yours. Love always. Graham.*"

"What was the date on that letter?" Maggie asked, wiping the tears from her face.

Ellie turned it over and checked the top. "August 25, 1945."

"It didn't mention anything about my grandmother being pregnant."

Ellie held up a hand and read the letter again. "For someone in love like he seemed to be, he would have been over the moon."

"Well, now we know she didn't tell him," Maggie said. "And this was his only letter to her. He didn't answer any of her other letters, so maybe she thought he didn't want her anymore. And he never knew about my mom."

"But were there any other letters?" Ellie asked. "Did you find anything like that when you went through your grandmother's things?"

"No, not a thing." Maggie said.

"Well, she kept this scrapbook, she drew his picture, hid his letter and your mom's birth certificate. All together and bound. But why didn't they meet again?"

"Maybe he died in the war." Maggie felt a shiver run down her spine, even as the warm sun streamed in through the front window onto them.

They sat in silence for a few minutes before Maggie gathered up the documents and returned them to the back of the scrapbook. "Can you find him?"

"I can find almost anyone." Ellie pulled out her cell phone and shook her head regretfully. "If I had cell service, that is.

"Let's go." Maggie dashed out the door before Ellie could even get up, leaving her to lock the door behind them.

***

"You know," Ellie said as they drove towards Percyville at a speed that made her stomach flutter with anxiety. "This could be a great case for the seniors to get involved with. Do you mind if I call an emergency meeting for when we get back? "

Maggie glanced in her mirror and abruptly changed lanes.

Ellie grabbed the armrest and sucked in a breath. "Slow it down a bit, Mags. I want to arrive alive and all that."

Ellie's white face made Maggie check her speedometer and let out a gasp. "Jeebus! I'm so sorry, Ellie. My head is full of..."

"I get it." Ellie released her death grip on the armrest and adjusted her seat belt as the car slowed to the speed limit.

"Yes. Absolutely, call them." Maggie nodded in agreement. "They might have some good ideas, too."

For the next hour, Ellie called each of the seniors and gave them a brief update. Some wanted more information right away, but Ellie assured them all they'd discuss it when they got there. By the time she put her phone away, everyone had agreed to meet at the café.

"Our posse will be waiting for us when we get home." Ellie reached out and gave Maggie's arm a quick squeeze.

"But we might not find him, right?" Maggie asked, expecting the worst.

"No, we might not," Ellie answered. "But we have a full name, a date when he was in the war, and where he lived. That's a lot of good information to start with."

"But he's probably dead." Maggie sighed. "He'd be a gazillion years old."

"In his nineties, like Ruth and Shirley."

"Yeah, or he's married and has a family."

"So?"

They drove the rest of the way in silence until Maggie jerked in surprise. "That means if he has a family, *I* have a family!"

"Actually, it could." Ellie grinned as they pulled into the parking lot of the Cozy Corner Café. Ellie recognized Lenny and Doreen's cars. The other members of the group lived in the Tiny House Haven community behind the café and had probably walked over together. She opened the car door and turned to Maggie. "Are you okay? You don't have to do this."

Maggie picked up her purse and put her keys in a pocket. "I'm scared to death but I can't wait to see what we find."

They walked to the front door and Maggie caught her arm before she stepped inside. "My dad's going to flip when he hears what's going on."

"I doubt that." Ellie laughed. "He's going to love this!"

Chapter Twenty-Eight

When Maggie and Ellie walked in, they found the group in their seats, each with a cup in front of them. Daphne put a large pot of tea in the middle of the table.

"Cookies coming up," Daphne said to Maggie as Maggie put her purse away and thanked her before following Ellie into the back room.

The eager looks on the faces of the genealogy seniors were encouraging. Shirley greeted them, a hand rubbing her left hip as if to ease a pain. "Ruth is sorry she couldn't make it, but Jeremy is resting after his surgery. She won't leave his side."

Maggie nodded at her. "We're so glad she found Jeremy."

"But the rest of us are here and ready to help." Shirley guided Maggie to a chair, as if assisting someone who had suffered a massive shock.

Maggie and Ellie looked at each other in surprise. Shirley's growing concern for others, since Ruth's life had changed with Jeremy, had been startling, but in a good way.

"You'll have to give us some details," Phil said as he took a cookie from the plate Daphne had brought over. "This sounds complicated."

"Do you want to tell them?" Ellie asked Maggie.

Maggie leaned back in her chair. She took a minute to gather her thoughts. "So you all know that I inherited the Tavie Bakery, a farmhouse, and other miscellaneous items from a grandmother I didn't know was still alive."

Tess sighed. "I love those amazing baked goods, but they melt in your mouth and end up on your hips."

"Wow!" Doreen slapped the table in excitement. "I just realized you have *two* bakeries!"

"Not really," Maggie said. She took a deep breath and dove into the story. "I sold the majority interest in Tavie Bakery to the young couple who ran it for my grandmother. I'm keeping a substantial portion, but I want them to have free rein."

"That's very generous of you," Phil said.

"Or very silly," Lennie said.

"I can't run two places, and the Tavie Bakery is too big for me." Maggie looked around her café and back at her friends. "This café is everything I've ever wanted. I'm not greedy, and I've got some new recipes my grandmother left me."

"The winning pie recipe, by any chance?" Norma asked.

"That's one of them." Maggie smiled.

"Well, we can't wait to try the others," Lennie assured her.

"Tell them about the farmhouse," Ellie urged.

"Right," Maggie said. "My grandmother had a large farmhouse in the town where the Tavie Bakery is located."

"And she has a cute little cabin in the woods across a wooden bridge," Ellie said. "And acres and acres of land!"

"I still don't understand how you never knew her or that she was behind Tavie Bakery." Doreen said.

"My mother told me that her mother died when she was young. She never talked about her family. She said her father died in the war and she had no brothers or sisters."

"But she lied," Ellie stated.

"Oh, the lies we tell each other," Shirley muttered. "And ourselves." Everyone turned to her, but she refused to acknowledge their attention.

"Wait." Phil held up a hand. "What happened with the young man you thought threw the Molotov cocktail? Was he arrested?"

Maggie glanced frantically at Ellie, not sure how to respond.

"No," Ellie answered for her. "Francois was involved in a fatal car accident."

"Sweet Marie!" Lenny sat back in shock, a cookie halfway to his mouth. "There's more to this story than you're letting on, isn't there? This isn't a run of the mill "find someone" exercise, is it?"

"Well, it is now," Maggie assured him.

"Francois was causing Maggie a lot of problems," Ellie said. "Things weren't moving fast enough for him, and he was getting shifty."

"He broke into my grandmother's farmhouse and stole some things to sell," Maggie filled in. "But they were all returned."

The seniors waited for her to continue, and when she didn't, Shirley asked the pertinent question. "Okay, so how can we help you?"

"In the back of a scrapbook that my grandmother kept in the cabin, we found a letter from a man I believe to be my grandfather. He was there for a month during the war, and that is another story. Their love story is quite sad, but there's a chance he's still alive."

"And he doesn't know about you?" Tess asked, a hand to her heart at the thought.

"He does not." Maggie shook her head.

"But how do you figure where to start?" Doreen asked. "I mean, this was what, the mid-forties? What information do you have to find him?"

"Well." Ellie took over from Maggie, who picked up a cookie. "We ran into a friend of Octavie's in St. Anne de Lafont. Her name is Louise Ethier, and she told us what she knew. Then we found Octavie's diary, and figured out the whole story. We found Maggie's mom's birth record on Drouin and the actual certificate at the cabin. All information confirms that his name is Graham Brodie, he came from Moose River in New Brunswick, and he had just become a doctor and was about to start his own practice when the war began. After his month here with Octavie, he had to go back to the war. Now, either their wires got crossed, he was injured, or died, but they never saw each other again."

"You mean Octavie never told him about your mom?" Shirley asked Maggie.

"Not that I'm aware of," Maggie said.

"So, your mother grew up without a father?" Lenny asked.

"She did," Maggie said. "She thought he died in the war."

"Maybe he did," Phil said.

"Maybe," Maggie mumbled.

"And maybe he didn't!" Norma rubbed her hands together. "Where do we start, Ellie?"

"Like we did when we tried to find Jeremy for Ruth?" Phil asked as he started up his laptop. "The WWII records at the Library and Archives Canada, right?"

They all stared at Phil in shock as he typed one finger at a time across the keyboard. Phil was notably not tech-savvy, but to see him squint at the screen as he typed in the website address was both shocking and wonderful. He looked around to find everyone looking at him.

"What? I met a nice young man at the computer store, and he told me what I needed. I've been using Google to figure things out. This Google thing is amazing."

Shirley squeezed his shoulder. "You're amazing, Phil. I'm delighted to see that."

Phil blushed at her attention, everyone else sneaking glances at each other.

"Yes," Ellie said. "That's the site. Let's start with the file called Service Files of the Second World War - War Dead, 1939-1947."

"Why not search the main files of all servicemen?" Lennie asked.

"Because they're restricted." Ellie reached for a cookie. "The records of the war dead are open for anyone to search. So, if he's not in those files, we assume he made it through the war."

"Like Jeremy did." Shirley nodded her understanding.

"And if he didn't die then, we can move on."

Phil typed with his index fingers, and it was obvious he had practiced because he moved quickly. "What's his name again?"

"Graham Brodie," Maggie said. She held her breath as he typed, praying that her grandfather's name would not be in the records.

"Nope," Phil said. He looked at Ellie for further instructions.

"Is it time for Facebook?" Tess asked. "Speaking of which, I found a cousin on Facebook last week."

"Oh, dear." Lennie turned to his wife. "Not Rachel. Please tell me it wasn't Rachel."

"Well." Tess hesitated when she saw Lennie shake his head. "I didn't get in touch with her because the pictures and posts were a little—"

"Out there?" Lennie asked.

"She hasn't changed," Tess admitted.

Phil looked up again and frowned. "There are two Graham Brodies in New Brunswick, none that would be his age."

"But we need to check them out to see if they're his son or grandson," Ellie said.

Maggie leaned in closer to Phil as he scrolled through the entries. "None of these looks like him. And they've got their sites set to private, so we can't look at other pictures." Her shoulders slumped.

"It's possible he's not on Facebook," Doreen said. "A lot of older people don't even use computers." Everyone turned to Phil.

"Better late than never." Phil held up his hands to acknowledge the remark.

"Okay," Ellie said. "Let's go with the 411 search for a phone number. It's a long shot, but we'll give it a try, and then go to Ancestry."

Phil's two fingers flew over the keys as he brought up the 411.ca website and typed Graham's name into the box. "Should I type in New Brunswick too?"

"Yes," Maggie said. She squirmed in her seat, desperate to find something that would link her to Graham, other than her mother's birth certificate.

"What town did you say he was from?" Phil asked, looking over the top of the laptop at Ellie.

"Moose..." Ellie started.

"River," Phil finished for her, a huge grin spreading across his face.

They all sat, stunned.

"Are you saying there's a phone number for Graham Brodie in Moose River?" Maggie whispered.

"Yes." Phil grabbed a pen and paper and wrote down the number, handing it to her. "And what are the chances he even still lives there at all?" he asked, always the one to bring everyone back to reality. "He could have moved or..."

Ellie nodded. "We get it Phil; we just need a place to start."

"He could have gone back there because he told my grandmother that's where he came from. Maybe he wanted her to find him and didn't want to move away," Maggie said. "And maybe *he* thought *she* had changed her mind."

"That's so romantic," Doreen gushed, her hands clasped on the table, her attention laser-focused on the drama unfolding before her. "Can you imagine someone doing this?"

Tess turned to her husband, Lennie, and smiled. "Yes, I can. We express love in all sorts of different ways." He patted her leg affectionately under the table.

But Maggie had pulled out her cell phone and was dialing. Everyone sat frozen, not wanting to disturb her concentration. She put the call on conference so they all could hear.

An old man answered. "Hello?"

"Hello. Is this Graham Brodie?" Maggie's voice trembled with excitement.

"Yes, who's this?" He sounded confused and worried.

"My name is Maggie Williams. I live in Quebec."

"Quebec?" They heard his breath catch.

"Did you know an Octavie Duprat?"

"Oh, my goodness." Graham's words were a whisper, almost a groan. "Who are you?"

"I'm her granddaughter."

"You're the daughter of the little girl I saw her with," he whispered.

"You saw my mother? When?" Maggie asked, leaning towards the phone.

"About five years after the war," he said. "I had been injured, and my memory was fuzzy for a long time. It took me all those years to get in any kind of shape to go looking for Octavie. To have anything worthwhile to offer her."

"Why didn't you talk to her when you saw her?" Maggie's arms were wrapped tightly around her stomach, as if dreading the words that would come next.

"Because she had obviously moved on. She had a child, a husband," he sighed. "I wasn't going to step in and mess up her life."

"She never had a husband," Maggie told him.

"But..." Graham sucked in a deep breath that everyone in the Cozy Corner could hear.

The group around the table sat frozen, waiting for Maggie to tell him.

"Florence, my mother, was your daughter," Maggie said softly. "And Octavie thought something had happened to you."

"Florence?" Graham said. "That was my mother's name."

"I know."

The silence stretched to an uncomfortable length before Graham spoke again. "I think we need to talk, young lady."

"Indeed, we do!" Maggie smiled, glancing at the friends around the table.

"What are the chances of us meeting?"

Chapter Twenty-Nine

It took two days to arrange the details. Daphne would take care of the Café, and Quinn would be happy to babysit Cali.

At 5:00 a.m. on the day of the trip, with the sun barely peeking through the sky, Maggie and Ellie piled into Maggie's car and headed out for their six-hour drive.

The smell hit Ellie as soon as she buckled up, and she grabbed the bag from the backseat. "When did you bake these? They're still hot!"

"I made a few things for Daphne before I left."

"But your normal baking time is six in the morning," Ellie put the bag to her nose and took a deep whiff.

"So, I got up a little earlier today." Maggie rescued the bag from her friend in hopes of delaying the coming snack raid — at least until they hit the highway.

"I hope you have coffee." Ellie turned to look at the other things on the backseat, then settled back.

"Happy?" Maggie asked as they reached the entrance to the secondary highway.

"Thermos, check!" Ellie pulled out her phone and opened the map application. "So, have you figured out how to get there? I see you don't have your GPS device." She motioned to the bare dashboard where the gift she had given Maggie should have been installed.

"You know I prefer the old way," Maggie said, checking her rear-view mirror. "I went over the map last night and wrote out all the directions."

Ellie stared at her like she was a unicorn. She waved her phone in the air, the screen showing a map with directions. "Will you let me lead the way with technology? I mean, you can't look at your notes and drive at the same time."

Maggie gave her a quick grin. "I knew you'd want to handle this part of the trip. And no, I have no problem with it."

Ellie checked the phone and enlarged the map with her fingers. "So, we take the fifteen to the six-forty and then the forty all the way to – oh, we're going through Trois-Rivieres!"

"Does that have a special meaning for you?"

"No, I just like the name."

"Jeesh! You are such a weirdo!"

"And you love me," Ellie gave her a big smile and turned back to her phone. "And we cross the St. Lawrence just before Quebec City."

"We're not going through?" Maggie sounded disappointed.

"No. Have you never been there?"

"No," Maggie said, setting the car to a comfortable cruising speed in the light traffic. "I've always wanted to visit the older part of the city. Do the tourist thing."

"We could stop there for a break, it looks like the halfway point."

"Maybe we'll save it and come back another time. I'm too nervous to enjoy being a tourist today."

"Fair enough. Then we follow Highway 20 to Saint Patrice and make a hard right onto the eighty-five down to Moose River. Easy peasy."

"Just a long drive," Maggie sighed.

"But we'll be along the river a lot and take our time. Enjoy the view."

"Thanks for coming, Ellie," Maggie said quietly. "I'm nervous about meeting him. What if he doesn't like me? Or he's mad about how my grandmother..." She glanced at Ellie, eyes wide. "I can't believe she was alive all this time. It upsets me that my mom cut her off and my grandmother let it happen!"

Ellie touched her arm and gave it a gentle squeeze. "Easy there, Mags. We have no idea what was going on in her life during all this. Maybe it *was* for the best.

You may never know the whole truth. But as far as your grandfather is concerned, I think you should grab this experience with both hands and enjoy every minute. How wonderful for you to find him, for however long you have. Look at Ruth and Jeremy. Gosh, they're in their nineties and who knows how long they've got left, but they're stuck together like glue now and I've never seen Ruth so happy."

"But..."

"No buts," Ellie said. "I understand your fears, I really do. But that's just the story in your head. You have nothing to go on. You and Graham were both in a position where you had no say in the matter."

Maggie let out a huge sigh and fumbled for her sunglasses in the tray between the seats. The sun was just peaking and it would be a blinding drive for the next hour as they drove into Montreal. At this point, all she wanted to do was get through the city and off the island.

Traffic was surprisingly light, and the drive along the St. Lawrence River calming. As they neared Quebec City, they found a place off the highway to stop, near the bridge they would take to the other side of the river. They pulled into the parking lot just before lunch, and walked along the winding path to Gagnon Beach. With Maggie's baked goods in hand, they found a spot by the water where they sat and watched the traffic on the river. The sun was warm and while stretching out in the sand would have felt wonderful, they helped each other up and back to the car.

Ellie took over the driving, and while she hated highway driving, she knew exactly where she was going, which made the stress easier to handle. Soon they were passing through farmland, smelling the river through the open windows.

"Look over there." Maggie pointed to a sign along the highway that stated that Grosse Ile was nearby. Ellie took a quick look, then focused on the road. "I've always wanted to go there. I can't imagine what it must have been like for so many immigrants to land there and never leave. So many people arrived sick. It must have been terrible."

"Most of the immigrants were Irish, fleeing the famine of 1845-1849. Grosse Ile had a quarantine station and everything. But, fun fact, the government had already set up the island to contain a cholera epidemic that came with a lot of European immigrants years before."

"I didn't know that," Maggie said. "You would have made a good teacher."

"I doubt it, but history is my jam! And I think I see a theme emerging here." Ellie laughed. "Why don't you make a note of all the places we pass that we want to visit, and we'll take a girls' trip in the fall."

Maggie took out her little notebook and started scribbling. "That's a great idea."

They stopped along the way for a real lunch, and arrived shortly after at the quaint motel where they would be staying for the next two nights.

Ellie got out and stretched, her back aching from being stuck in the driver's seat. They headed to the office together, feeling good about their choice of accommodations the moment they stepped inside and saw the elderly lady behind the reception desk.

"Can I help you?" she asked. "My name is Judy Holmes, and I own the Shady Hills Motel." She closed the cover of a woodcarving magazine she had been reading, and Ellie could just make out a sharp knife and a piece of wood on the desk next to Judy. The top half looked like the beginning of a bear. The woman caught Ellie's raised eyebrow and held up the half finished creation. "New hobby. Got to keep your hands moving these days. Use it or lose it, as the saying goes."

"We have a room reserved for the next two nights," Maggie said. "The names are McLellan and Williams."

"Ah, yes." The woman ran a finger down the page of her ledger and turned to take a key from the back wall. "It's the biggest one, at the end. Even has a back porch. Well, they all do, but yours looks out into the woods."

Maggie took the key and pulled out her wallet.

"Oh, heavens no." Judy shook her head. "Graham paid for the room, dear."

Ellie and Maggie were stunned. Did this woman know what they were doing here? "You know Graham Brodie?" Maggie asked quietly.

"Everybody knows Dr. Brodie, dear," Judy said. "He insisted you have the best room."

"How did he know where we were staying?" Ellie asked.

"Not to be one to toot my own horn," the woman grinned, "but the Shady Hills Motel is the only place to stay for miles and miles, and we have never had a negative review!"

"Well, that's something to be proud of," Ellie said. "Thank you."

As they turned to leave, the woman called out. "Oh, and there's a vending machine on the way, healthy drinks and snacks."

They moved the car closer to their room and hauled their bags inside. It was nice. Two queen size beds with earth-colored bedspreads, a desk and chair, a large TV, a small kitchenette with a coffee maker and a refrigerator underneath. Which Ellie promptly opened and pulled out some chocolate bars.

"Do we have to pay for these?" Maggie asked.

"I don't know if it's like those expensive hotels."

"You mean any hotel?"

Ellie didn't answer, but unwrapped a Mars bar and took a bite. "I love these!"

Maggie sat on her chosen bed; her shoulders drooped. "What now? Should we call him and let him know we're here?"

"We should," Ellie sat next to her. "But I'm sure Judy has already informed Dr. Brodie of our arrival."

They looked at each other and laughed out loud.

"It's like an old movie, isn't it? Arriving at the manor to meet long-lost relatives, afraid of being sent back to the poorhouse."

"You really do have a crazy imagination!" Ellie said.

***

Maggie hung up the phone, stood up and stretched. Neither of them was used to such long car rides. "He'd like to see us as soon as we can get there." She handed Ellie a piece of paper. "His address and directions."

Ellie pulled out her phone and entered the address, and within minutes she had a map in front of her showing how to get to Graham's home. "Should take us about ten minutes."

Maggie opened her suitcase and pulled out a plastic bag.

"Presents?" Ellie asked.

"You'll see." Maggie grabbed the car keys and left Ellie to lock the room. Within minutes, they were consulting Ellie's map and heading down the road.

They only made one wrong turn, and as they pulled into Graham's driveway, the view was breathtaking. And surprising.

"It's a farm!" Maggie said.

They sat in the car for a minute, looking at the small farmhouse, the red-roofed barn, the chicken coop, and the orchard.

"It looks like..." Ellie started.

"Like my grandmother's place."

The slam of the front door startled them, and they hurried out to meet the older man who was making his way toward them.

His gait was steady, if slow. He had a full head of white hair, and was clean shaven. His clothes looked freshly pressed. His arms were outstretched toward Maggie, his smile wavering as he reached her and pulled her in close for a hug.

"You look just like her," he murmured into her hair before stepping back, overwhelmed by Maggie's appearance.

Ellie handed him a tissue and he wiped away his tears. "Thank you, Miss?"

Ellie held out her hand. "I'm Ellie McLellan, this one's best friend." She motioned to Maggie beside her, who had not moved an inch since she had been wrapped in her grandfather's arms.

"Maggie, dear," he reached up to touch her hair. "Are you okay?"

"Yes," she whispered. "No, not really. I didn't know anything about you, or my grandmother until a short while ago."

"Amazing, isn't it?" he asked, his smile lighting up his face again and leaving Ellie in no doubt as to whose grandfather he was. He had a crease down the left side of his mouth that was identical to Maggie's.

"Yes." Maggie hesitated then threw her arms around her grandfather's neck and held on tight. "I'm so happy to meet you."

"Me too." Graham pulled back and took her hand, leading her into the house. "Inside, both of you. Out of this sun and heat."

They entered a cool hallway where a black mutt of a dog sat patiently, its tail wagging wildly as they approached.

"And this is Mabel," Graham announced, nodding to the dog. The dog ran up and sat down in front of them with a plop, and raised a paw.

"Oh, my goodness!" Ellie crouched down and shook Mabel's paw, giving her a great head rub as well. "I wish my dog did that!"

"Quinn might have her trained by the time we get back." Maggie laughed. She, too, bent down to meet Mabel. And when the introductions were over, the dog headed down the hall and disappeared into a kitchen at the far end.

"This way, ladies." Graham followed Mabel, and they found her curled up in a well-worn dog bed next to a deep-cushioned rocking chair by the fireplace in the corner. "She lies there all year round, whether it's cold or not. She's getting older now, just like me, and this is our spot. Have a seat."

After motioning them to take seats around the oak wood table, he retrieved glasses of lemonade from the refrigerator and brought them to the table. "I have to admit, I was so nervous all morning that I made this from scratch. The first batch was terrible, but Judy talked me through it. Let me know what you think."

Ellie and Maggie took sips and were pleasantly surprised by the taste, tangy and sweet at the same time. "This is exactly what we needed," Maggie said.

Graham sat down with them and rested his arms on the table, never taking his eyes off Maggie. "I can't believe I have a granddaughter! You have no idea how much you look like O at your age." He shook his head in amazement. He took her hand again, obviously not wanting to let go of this new connection. "So, tell me about yourself. And Octavie, please."

Ellie sat back and watched them talk for the next hour. Maggie shared bits and pieces of her life, told him about her mother, the shock of finding out about Octavie, and the joy of discovering family. She gave Ellie all the credit for her genealogical detective work, but Ellie just smiled.

When the conversation died down, Maggie pulled the bag she had brought from the floor to the table. "And I wanted to return something to you, and share something I think – I hope, will make you happy." She pulled out the green plaid shirt that had lived in the cabin for decades and handed it to him. "It might smell, because I don't think my grandmother ever washed it, and I didn't want to either."

"Oh, my goodness!" Graham took the shirt and put it to his nose. "Do you smell the flowers?" He held it out to Maggie and she took a small sniff. She frowned, sneezed, and took a deeper sniff. "Lilacs," he said. "Her favorite." He held the shirt and shook his head, his eyes welling once more. "What happened?" he whispered.

Maggie took another item from the bag and placed it in front of him.

Ellie gasped and then smiled. "Of course! How appropriate."

"This is my grandmother's diary," Maggie said, pushing it towards him. "It starts just before the farm was used as a way-station for soldiers, and ends shortly after Florence is born. But I think you'll find all the answers in there."

At first, he didn't want to touch the diary. He stared at it as if weighing whether he wanted to know or not.

Maggie stood up. "Ellie and I are going to take a walk around your beautiful property and we'll be back in a bit." She hugged him from behind and walked out the back door, Ellie at her heels.

When they returned, Graham was sitting in his rocking chair by the fire, Mabel fast asleep by his side. Octavie's journal rested on his lap, his hand holding it tightly.

Maggie and Ellie returned to their seats and waited for him to speak, unsure of his reaction.

"Life is funny," he said softly. "Octavie was my first love. When I thought she had married another, I was heartbroken. But by then I was on my way to having a medical practice and felt I should put those thoughts behind me. I loved my life. I loved being a doctor and helping my community. I fell in love with a wonderful woman and we had a good life together. You would have liked her."

Maggie smiled, but let him continue his tale.

"We weren't blessed with children, but that was okay, because I had all these families to take care of. I saw the children through good and bad times. It was a very tight community." He paused and stared at Maggie. "And now I have you. I guess we'll both need some time to take it all in. How long are you here for?"

He seemed worried, and Maggie rushed to assure him. "We're here for two nights."

"Not nearly enough time," he frowned.

"But I can come back, and you can come visit me in Percyville."

"And you're a baker you say?"

"The best baker," Ellie chimed in. "She gets it from her grandmother!"

"We have whatever time left we want to have," Graham said, getting up and reaching for her hand. "Come walk with me. I want to tell you about your grandmother."

Ellie sat on the balcony, Mabel at her side, as she watched her best friend and her grandfather head off down the path.

Maggie turned to her. "Ellie! I have a whole family to learn about!" She entwined her arm through her grandfather's and they headed out into the woods.

About Author

Beth Farrar has been writing stories since her parents handed her a library card. And encouragement from English teachers set her on a serious path of learning the craft.

From writing TV scripts to full length movies for pleasure and practice, she developed her writing skills by exploring various mediums. Filling notebooks with ideas, sketching characters and locations, and inventing sticky situations for characters to survive, is Beth's happy place (besides walking in cemeteries, but that's another story).

For fifteen years Beth wrote a monthly column, Living Country, in her local English language newspaper, Main Street, sharing interesting observations of living and raising her three sons in the country with her husband. Having always loved genealogy, Beth melded two of her passions together and created the Ellie McLellan Genealogy Mystery series.

For tips and tricks on how to write your own personal history story, head over to Beth Farrar – Author on Facebook for more information or head to her website to sign up to her newsletter and receive a free Oral History Questions to help you start writing your own personal history.

bethfarrar.com

Afterword

Would you like to write your own personal story? Feel free to head over to my Instagram page at "bethfarrar8115", or my Facebook site at "Beth Farrar – Author". You'll find more tips about how to start putting together your own life story, or head to my website to sign up to my newsletter and receive a free Oral History Questions to help you start writing your own personal history. bethfarrar.com

The seniors in Ellie's genealogy group learned a couple of things during this story that you can apply to your own journey.

1. Google is your friend! If you are looking for a person, place or thing, take a look at what Google can find for you – and take a screenshot of anything you might want to refer to later. You may be surprised by what you find, and where you find it.

2. Census returns – check out the most recent available and see if you can find your parents, or you might be old enough to appear on one!

3. Draw a floorplan of homes you've lived in (check old photos if you've forgotten what some of them looked like).

4. Update or get a Will made! I'm serious, this is important!!

Acknowledgments

Once again I start by thanking my amazing editor, Ronnie Roberts. Without your initial suggestions and guidance, growth could not have taken place!

My main reader, Teresa O'Neil, your ability to "hear" my voice is stunning, and I thank you for all your suggestions, no matter how reluctant you were to give them. Please keep doing that!

My eagle eyed proofreader, Daphne Petersen, who always comes through with those little mistakes that readers would hate to read. Being able to catch those beforehand is a relief for all!

My three sons, Liam, Connar, and Devlin, your cheering from the sidelines keeps a smile on my face.

And my hubby, through thick and thin you've always encouraged me to be realistic and never give up on my dreams. I thank you for not losing patience when I suddenly jump up and run to make notes on an idea! You mean the world to me.

Family Crimes - Book 4

If you enjoyed following Ellie McLellan and her group of senior genealogists solve their mystery, get ready for their next adventure.

The subject is family crimes.

The time is fall.

The senior genealogist group is heading out for a short vacation to help Norma uncover the truth about a family crime that was never solved.

Will the seniors survive a trip together, and will one of them fulfill a dream of their lifetime?

Norma is determined to set things straight, with the help of her neice, Ellie McLellan, and her fellow senior genealogists. Revealing the truth will cause ripples in her family but justice has to be served.

But will it be too late to right the wrong?

Printed in Great Britain
by Amazon

24354779R00116